THE

Winds

FROM

Further West

THE

Winds

FROM

Further West

Alexander
McCall Smith

PANTHEON BOOKS   *New York*

FIRST U.S. HARDCOVER EDITION
PUBLISHED BY PANTHEON BOOKS 2025

Published by Pantheon Books, a division of Penguin Random
House LLC, 1745 Broadway, New York, NY 10019. Originally
published in hardcover in Great Britain by Polygon, an imprint
of Birlinn Ltd, in 2024.

Pantheon Books and colophon are registered trademarks of
Penguin Random House LLC.

Library of Congress Cataloging-in Publication Data
Name: McCall Smith, Alexander, [date] author.
Title: The winds from further West / Alexander McCall Smith.
Description: First American edition. | New York : Pantheon Books, 2025.
Identifiers: LCCN 2024037235 | ISBN 9780385551410 (hardcover) |
    ISBN 9780385551434 (ebook)
Subjects: LCGFT: Novels.
Classification: LCC PR6063. C326 W55 2025 |
    DDC 823/.914—dc23/eng/20240812
LC record available at https://lccn.loc.gov/2024037235

penguinrandomhouse.com | pantheonbooks.com

Book design by Anna B. Knighton

Printed in the United States of America
1st Printing

The authorized representative in the EU for product safety
and compliance is Penguin Random House Ireland, Morrison
Chambers, 32 Nassau Street, Dublin D02 YH68, Ireland,
https://eu-contact.penguin.ie.

This book is for

A l i s t a i r   M o f f a t ,

who has brought the delights
of Scottish history to so many.

PART

One

One

Almost everything starts in a small way. There is no shortage of examples—and attendant metaphors: rivers begin with a trickle of water in a remote upland; oaks emerge from nothing bigger than an acorn; a cloud the size of a hand becomes a full-blown storm. Often it is an apparently insignificant event that ends up dictating the whole shape of our lives: a random, even whimsical, decision; an unanticipated remark; a chance encounter—any of these may have consequences far beyond the immediate.

For Neil, just such a moment occurred when he walked into a Turkish barbershop in Glasgow. He had made an appointment, but he was early, and he had to wait. Had he been on time, his life would probably have been quite different. As it was, he sat down on one of the cracked-leather-covered seats and picked up a copy of *New Scientist* left by a previous customer among the usual detritus of the barbershop: the men's grooming monthlies, the well-thumbed copies of car magazines, the out-of-date newspapers. *New Scientist* was a cut above all that; it reported on scientific advances: new non-stick saucepans, gene editing, insights into the earth's crust. It also carried advertisements for scientific jobs, and it was one of these that caught his eye. An Edinburgh research institute had a vacancy for a medically qualified researcher. That was what Neil was, and he was coming to the end of his public-health contract in Glasgow. He was thirty-five, and ready for a change. The timing could not have been better, and Neil was appointed after an interview that proved surprisingly cursory. He was, in fact, the only candidate, although they kept that from him, out of consideration for his feelings.

Although independent of the major local university, and not part of any other Scottish university, the institute ran courses for undergraduate students, participated in doctoral programmes, and undertook research for government bodies. Its staff were experts in both animal and human health; they tracked the progress of diseases at home and abroad, recording their waxing and waning with the seasons and the movement of animals and of people. They responded to the occasional scare, as swine or avian flu wove their way in and out of the newspaper headlines. They watched, at a distance, outbreaks of cholera in distant shanty towns. They waited for what many of them thought to be inevitable: Ebola and Marburg fever were lurking in the wings. It was potentially apocalyptic work.

"Will microbes get us eventually?" a friend asked him. "That's what you do, isn't it? That's the question that you're paid to answer."

Neil smiled. "They've been trying hard enough," he replied. "And yes, they probably will—sooner or later. But they won't necessarily get all of us. That happened with the Neanderthals, I think, but we might dodge that bullet."

His friend was curious, and Neil explained further. "Neanderthals probably died out because they had no resistance to the diseases that *Homo sapiens* brought when we met them."

"Rather like the Aztecs?"

"Yes. They had no resistance to Old World viruses. It was an unequal battle. Neanderthals may have had the same experience."

"So they didn't die because they couldn't compete with us—and our clever ways?"

Neanderthals were not stupid, Neil pointed out. They used tools and had fire. They even appeared to engage in artistic activity. Their bad press, which portrayed them as brutes, was almost certainly wide of the mark.

Such speculation—historical epidemiology—was, he said, the intellectually challenging part of the subject. For the most part, as he was at pains to point out, his job was much more mundane: gathering statistics, preparing tables, tracking the progress of winter flu as it spread across the globe, following the paths it had always followed—those of humanity on the move. "If only we would stay put for a while," Neil observed, "we'd run into fewer hostile organisms. But we won't. Humanity won't change. Humanity *can't* change."

That was a rare defeatist moment. For the most part, he saw no point in dwelling upon the bleak aspects of his work. He, and people like him, might do little to change the basic rules of engagement between human beings and microbes, but here and there, in small corners of the battlefield, they achieved their largely unsung victories. And in the background, their research, sometimes painfully slow and seemingly entirely theoretical, built up the human armoury against microbial defeat.

Neil had barely been in his new post in Edinburgh for three months when he met Chrissie Thomson. She was a junior colleague at the institute, a microbiologist with a special interest in respiratory infections. She was on a postdoctoral research fellowship that had another year to run before further funding would need to be found. That did not worry her: Chrissie, it became clear, had money, having inherited from a childless relative an expensive flat in

London. Having no desire to live in it, she had sold this for a figure that Neil found difficult to believe.

"How can anyone afford to pay that?" he had asked. "And who would want to anyway? Think what you could do with that sort of money."

"You could live in London," Chrissie said, smiling. "That's what those places cost."

"But . . . three bedrooms . . . That's more than a million per bedroom."

"It's the area," said Chrissie. "Mayfair, no less."

He shook his head. "What are you doing having relatives who live in Mayfair? Nobody *real* lives there any longer."

"She was very old. She'd lived there for decades—before it became out of reach for anybody who actually paid taxes in this country."

"I suppose so." He paused. "Do you think it's honest money they paid? The people who bought it from you, I mean."

Chrissie said she had not met them. "They live in Monte Carlo."

"Then it's not."

"Possibly. But we had no way of telling and you shouldn't refuse to sell a flat to somebody just because they live in a place like that."

"Like Monte Carlo?"

"Yes. I wouldn't live there—and I suspect you wouldn't either. But presumably there are *some* people who aren't there for tax avoidance reasons."

Neil looked doubtful. "I don't know. You may be right."

"Anyway, I don't think they're going to spend much time in London. My solicitor said that they were far too busy."

He looked away. "What are you going to do with all that money?"

"Nothing at the moment. When my postdoc runs out, I suppose I'll live on it—until I get something else. It removes the urgency from my life."

"You're very lucky." He paused. "But you still want to work?"

She gave him a sideways look. "Of course I do."

He sensed that he was being reproached. "I was just wondering how ambitious you were."

Chrissie frowned. "I'm as ambitious as . . . anybody else."

He pointed out that in academic circles that could amount to ruthlessness. "They'd murder for a chair," he said. "An American poet. It was one of those lines that stuck, for some reason."

She looked at him with interest. "I didn't know you liked poetry."

"I do. Some of it lodges in the mind, and comes back at odd times. People say that the thing about poetry is its power to haunt."

She looked thoughtful. "I'm just a simple scientist. Perhaps you're too clever for me."

He denied that he was clever. "I'm nothing special. An ordinary doctor."

"You shouldn't be too modest," she said. "You have a post in a prestigious institute. You can do research. There are plenty of people who would like to be where you are."

"As Robert Lowell pointed out . . ." He paused. "But you wouldn't do anything to get where you want to get, would you?"

She smiled. "I wouldn't murder for a chair, if that's what you're asking."

"Of course you wouldn't."

She became serious. "People don't expect women to be as ambitious as men, do they? And yet why shouldn't we want the things that men have?"

He said that he saw no reason why it should be any different for women. "Lady Macbeth was the ruthless one—Macbeth himself was the wimp."

Now she changed the subject. "I admit that having a bit of money gives me freedom. That's something, I suppose."

"It is. For most people, that would be just about everything."

She did not respond to this, but she looked at him. "Do you care about money? Does it mean much to you?"

He wondered whether there was a barb in her question. Did she think that he might be interested in her for her money?

He shook his head. "Not particularly," he said. "Money's useful if there's something you want to do that you wouldn't otherwise be able to afford. Sure, it must be nice to have it then. But otherwise . . ." He shrugged. "I'm fairly indifferent to it."

She looked pleased. "I was hoping you'd say that."

"As long as I have enough of it," he added.

A month or so after their first date—dinner at a seafood restaurant in Leith—Chrissie announced that she had been looking at a flat on the south side of the city. "It has views," she said. "And acres of space. We could each have two rooms."

He was surprised. "Are you asking me to live with you?"

She blushed. "I suppose I was. I have a habit of thinking out loud. Perhaps I was just thinking of what a good idea it would be."

He smiled at her. "Why not? We all have to live somewhere."

His response helped her to overcome her embarrassment. "That's a very romantic way of putting it."

He was quick to apologise. "I'm sorry. Of course I'd like to live with you—who wouldn't?"

"Oh, I suspect a lot of people wouldn't. I'm a bit untidy."

He said that he wouldn't mind. He was untidy too.

"And I take hours in the shower," she continued. "Hours."

"I very rarely shower." He laughed.

She looked at him with mock reproach. "And you a doctor too . . . with all you know about germs. Perhaps I should reconsider my invitation."

"Please don't."

"All right. Let's move in together. As long as you shower regularly."

He gave her his hand to shake. Then he kissed her.

She said, "We're going to be so happy. I can feel it."

"So can I."

He thought: I'm saying that without thinking. He was not completely sure that he would be happy living with her, but, at the same time, he had no reason to think that he would be unhappy. That did not mean that he was indifferent to her: what he felt was fondness—and it was a growing fondness at that. It could mature into a deeper love, but until it did that, it was what one might call a satisfactory relationship. That was the lot of so many people who were in relationships that might not be passionate or exhilarating, but that were satisfactory enough . . . *Satisfactory*: such faint praise, such a second prize . . . And yet, for most people, that is all that came their way in this life. They lived in hope of being swept off their feet, but that did not happen, and they accepted it. It was not so bad being *a bit in love*, or *in love to an extent*.

Life, for most people, was something that just happened to them. They were not the authors of the script—it was simply there, and they read out the part allotted to them. And in the background, like the clockwork that kept the whole thing going, was simple chance. It occurred to Neil then that had he not walked into that Turkish barbershop he would not be here: he would not have met Chrissie and they would not be planning to live together. They might even end up getting married—because that was what people who lived together often did. Although neither had said anything about that yet. If they did, of course, then his choice of life partner would have been determined by the sheer chance of needing a haircut at that particular time. He reminded himself that that was probably the same for just about everything that happened to us. We imagined that our lives were shaped by choices we made: it was not like that at all, or only to a limited extent. Our lives were the creations of chance, of hazard, of events that in many cases took place long before our conception. We were old business, warmed up for a new present and an uncertain future. But that understanding, although unsettling to some, should not necessarily detract from any pleasure that we might take in life, and at that moment, Neil knew that he was content. He had an interesting and secure job; he was in a stable relationship with a woman whom most people would regard as something of a catch; and he had somewhere to live. If he had to sit down and write out a list of things he needed but did not have, he would have been hard-pressed to come up with anything. The Turkish barbershop in Glasgow had done him proud.

Chrissie's bid for the flat was successful, and they moved in two months later. They chose their furniture together, equipping it with an eclectic mixture of Victorian and modern. Chrissie discovered that she enjoyed browsing in antiques warehouses, and came up with a series of bargains—items that others would not wish to clutter their houses with but which looked just right, she said, in their late nineteenth-century flat. She took time off to go to auctions, and came back with objects for which Neil saw little use: a Victorian what-not stand, a folding campaign desk, an American rocking chair that creaked with each movement. She bought books on oriental carpets and covered the floor with tribal art woven in some distant village. Neil smiled at all this: it was her flat and her money, and he approved of her colour sense.

They built up a circle of friends. Some of these were the squash players with whom Neil played every Friday evening; others were old school friends of Chrissie. One or two of them were people she had met at antiques fairs or auctions. They went to each other's houses for dinner at weekends; sometimes they went for walks together in the hills to the south of Edinburgh.

It was after one of these walks that Neil asked Chrissie if she was happy.

"Why ask that?" she responded.

He shrugged. "Because most of the time people don't think about how they feel about their lives. They just let them happen."

She frowned. "Do you think I'm unhappy? Is that what you think?"

"Of course not. I didn't say anything about you being unhappy. I merely wanted to know whether . . . everything was all right."

She gave him a sideways look. "Is it because my postdoc's almost expired?"

He shook his head. "No, I wasn't thinking about that." He paused. "That's not worrying you, is it?"

She assured him it was not. "I don't really care," she said. "In fact, I'm done with the way they fund science in this country. They force us to apply for grants every few years. Where's the job security in that?" She fixed him with a slightly accusing stare. "You don't have to worry. You're lucky. You have a permanent job. Not everybody has your luck."

He knew that he was fortunate. But he didn't want his good fortune to accentuate the uncertainties in her career, and her comment made him feel uncomfortable: he was prepared to accept that luck might play some part, but there was much more to it than that. He felt that he had his job because he had worked to achieve it: to say that he was lucky was to suggest that there had simply been a roll of the dice, and he had been fortunate enough to have guessed the right number. He looked at her, and wondered whether she thought that he had his job because of sheer chance rather than as through personal effort. She had no right to think that.

"Something will turn up," he said. "It always does."

He could tell that she was unconvinced.

"I doubt it," she said. "They're cutting back. And anyway, I'm not sure that I want to carry on with this job. What's the point?"

He was unprepared for this. "But I thought that microbiology was . . ."

She did not let him finish. "There are other ways of spending your life, you know. Microbiology's not the only thing."

"No," he said hesitantly. "It's not. But if you're a microbiologist, then isn't microbiology the thing you should be doing?"

She laughed. "There are hundreds of other careers. Hundreds."

He waited a few moments before saying, "What will you do instead?"

"I'm not saying that I'm going to do anything different. I may carry on being a microbiologist. I probably will. Or . . ."

She left the sentence unfinished.

"Or what?"

She waved a hand airily. "Or I could do something radically different. Interior decoration, for instance. I rather fancy that."

It was the first he had heard of that, and he waited for more of an explanation. She was looking at him, as if weighing up whether to say more. Evidently, she decided that she would. "I've been looking at a course."

He waited.

"It's part-time," she went on. "You can take the course at your own pace. You get a tutor. Mine's in Edinburgh. You meet online."

He was not sure what to say. Was she trying to tell him something—that she did not care? If she resented his success, then she might have wanted to do that. He could reassure her; he could say, "Look, I'm no threat to you." Or, "You don't have to prove anything to me." Something like that.

"You seem surprised," she said, after a while.

"Well, yes, I am—a bit. You never mentioned anything."

"Well, now I am," she said. "It's interesting. I like it. It's not microbiology."

"Well . . ."

"There's a case for developing entirely different skills," she said. "And, if I did have a career change, I could always go back later."

"Of course." He was doubtful, though. Science was competitive: those who went off, often found it impossible to get back in.

He looked at her. "Is the air full of the smoke of burning boats?" he asked.

She laughed. "Yes. Thick with it." And then she added, "You mustn't worry about it, Neil. Whatever happens, I'm not going to starve." She looked at him enquiringly. "Would you support me if I were broke? I mean, flat broke. Without a penny—literally."

He said that he would. Her enquiring look became one of bemusement. "You're so solid," she said.

He asked her what she meant by that.

"Nothing, really. I don't mean that you're . . . solid, in the sense of *heavy*. In fact, I don't think I meant to say it. Sorry."

"But you did think it?"

She turned away. "You mustn't try to read my thoughts," she said. "I was thinking of reliability, I suppose—you're reliable."

He held her gaze. "And you are too."

"Am I?" She did not seem convinced. Then she said, "Let's talk about something different."

They did, but he continued to think of this curious, unsettling conversation. He had the impression she was keeping something from him, but he was not sure what it might be. He had thought that there were few, if any, secrets you could conceal from a person you lived with; cohabitation, it seemed to him, was a particular form of nakedness. But perhaps he was wrong; perhaps that was wishful thinking. You could, he knew, fundamentally misunderstand the person with whom you lived; there were many who discovered that, to their dismay, even when they thought it inconceivable.

He asked himself: what if you stopped trusting those who were closest to you? He found it hard to imagine the chasm of utter loneliness that must open up once trust was lost. How could one sleep, knowing that the other might be awake, watching you, calculating, awaiting a chance to betray? Or laughing at you, perhaps, behind your back?

He put these thoughts out of his mind. They had simply talked about the possibility of doing something different; there was nothing essentially destabilising about that. Chrissie was experiencing what everyone felt when they came to the end of a postdoctoral contract. She would be wondering whether this was the end of her academic career and whether she would have to do something quite different—something for which she may feel herself unequipped. There would be lab work, of course, that was always available, but it tended to be routine and unrewarding in every sense—the equivalent of mundane work in a manufacturing industry. He could understand why she would view the prospect with foreboding.

T w o

The director of the institute was appointed by the university. When it was first set up, the institute had been run by a dean elected by the academic staff—a collegiate system that reflected the way in which most academic institutions had always been run. A managerial restructuring changed all that: the idea that people might choose academic leaders themselves was anathema to the authorities, who wanted a hierarchical structure of managers, each reporting up a clear chain of command all the way to the top. These managers would be appointed rather than chosen, and in this way, at a stroke, the democratic traditions of collegiate governance were consigned to history.

"We need to be nimble," the architect of the change argued. "We need to make quick decisions. We need to be able to respond to the academic and research marketplace. We're a business, after all—and businesses are in competition with other businesses."

"But look at universities—they were always run by professors," came the objection. "Why not now?"

"Because then was then, and now is now. It's a changed world."

When Neil first joined the institute, the last of the deans was still in office, but was due to retire within months. "The final surviving dinosaur," somebody said. "The last of those into whose room you could slip and talk about anything on your mind—without knocking, and without an appointment."

The dean had gone, walking out of the building on a Friday afternoon, missing the small reception that had been organised to mark his departure, because he found it too emotional, too painful. His younger colleagues knew how he felt, and did not blame him for missing his own party. They drank the wine that had been ordered by the institute secretary; one of them drank too much and inadvertently set off a fire extinguisher.

"You won't get away with that in future," a friend remarked. "You could do that under the ancien régime, but no longer. Watch out."

"It was rather nice, wasn't it?" said the miscreant. "Being a member of something rather than just an employee. Having colleagues who wouldn't blame you too much for setting off a fire extinguisher. I hardly touched it, you know."

The new director arrived the following week. She was called Henrietta Fold, was Irish—she had been a head of department at a university in Ireland—and was a bully. Her progress up the academic ladder had been impressive, fuelled by the ruthlessness she showed in her dealings with those both below and above her in the pecking order. Those who were below were lined up as allies or, if they failed to support her, sidelined at the first opportunity. Those who were above her were subjected to charm offensives so subtly managed that they usually failed to see what her motives were. They thought that Henrietta liked or admired them, but in reality, she was interested only in their usefulness to her in her ambitions.

Once she found herself in a position of power, she exercised it with determination—and indifference to the feelings of others. Those who objected to her decisions, or even merely questioned them, were subtly threatened with unpleasant consequences. In particular, when her support was needed for promotion—as it inevitably would be—a past failure to do as she bid would guarantee that such support would be denied. She made sure that people knew that; even if she did not spell it out in so many words, nobody was left in any doubt.

In extreme cases—where a member of staff might simply resist some policy proposed by Henrietta—she would bring in the support of students to intimidate them into compliance. This was done by Henrietta's cultivating of those student representatives who took the most radical line, and encouraging them to view her target as a reactionary threat to academic democracy. She was not the first authoritarian to use the enthusiasm of idealists for her own ends.

"Don't let anybody undo the progress you've made in dismantling the patriarchy," she said. "Resist. Expose them for what they are. Refuse your co-operation in our shared journey of discovery."

The journey of discovery to which she referred used to be described as education—a term that Henrietta discouraged from the beginning of her tenure of office.

"We are not here to educate young people," she announced at an early meeting with staff. "We are here to *share*. We are here to participate in the process of discovery that the students themselves will initiate and control."

"But the students don't know as much as we do," said a recently appointed lecturer in epidemiology. "I'm not saying that they're ignorant, or anything like that. I'm just saying that they haven't read the literature yet. They've not done . . . not done the stuff that we have. That's all."

Henrietta had fixed him with an icy stare. "I'm very sorry," she began, "but I must disagree profoundly with what you say. That's the old philosophy, if you can dignify it with the name. That's the position under which knowledge is seen as a commodity controlled by those who take it upon themselves to decide what others should know. That is the patriarchal top-down model that, frankly, will no longer be accepted in the academy."

The lecturer had stared at her in astonishment. Then he said, "But they don't know anything—or not very much—and if we don't teach them, then how are they going to learn? Sorry to be so obtuse, but how? I've just passed my driving test. I took lessons from this guy who showed me how to drive. I couldn't drive before I went to him." He paused. There were smiles on the faces of some of his colleagues; others remained impassive. "He didn't share anything with me—the instructor—he said you do it this way, see, and so I did. That's how I learned to drive."

There was an almost complete silence. A radiator in the background knocked quietly as the water coursed through its pipes. Nobody looked at one another.

Henrietta said, "We can discuss that some other time, Dr. Martin. Now is not appropriate."

"Good," Dr. Martin said. "Because I don't see how I can do my job unless I actually tell students how to do epidemiology. I have to *tell* them how to do it. *Tell* them."

Henrietta looked at the papers before her on the desk. There were people who were stuck in the past, and there were progressive people who were not. Those who were stuck *announced* themselves. It was risible, really: they might as well wear a badge.

Both Neil and Chrissie were at that meeting. They made a point of not sitting next to one another, as they had a tacit agreement to keep their private and professional lives apart. They occasionally exchanged glances, though, and did so at that meeting. Chrissie knew what Neil would be thinking, and he suspected that she felt much the same.

They discussed it over dinner. Neil said, "That woman's danger-ous. There are red lights flashing all over the place."

Chrissie shrugged. "She has her views."

He frowned. "Yes, dangerous views."

"That depends."

He stared at her. Henrietta could hardly have been cruder in her espousal of the new mantras. Did Chrissie not see how superficial the little homily had been? "Depends on what?"

"On your perspective. If you're interested in keeping things exactly as they were, then, yes, she's not going to stand for that, I imagine. But isn't that a good thing?"

He opened his mouth to say something, but she continued, "I know what she said seems a bit clichéd . . ."

"Seriously clichéd," he said.

"But look at the sentiment behind it."

"The sentiment?"

"Yes, the intention. What was she saying? That the old, autocratic ways of handing down knowledge had outlived their usefulness? That people want to have a say in what they learn?" She paused. "I can sign up to a lot of that. It's the democratisation of science."

He did not say anything immediately. She looked at him enquir-ingly.

"Are you okay with that?" she asked. "Surely you can see where she's coming from."

He looked up at the ceiling. "We still have to teach. What's the alternative? Will people learn things through a process of osmosis?"

"I think you're being too literal," said Chrissie. "All she's sug-gesting is a shading of approach. It's a subtle question."

For a few moments he was silent. Then he said, "She's intolerant. She has a view, and that's the only view she seems willing to accept."

"But you have a view, too. You're saying, aren't you, that your view is more compelling than hers."

"How are students going to learn?" he asked. "And are they going to decide the curriculum? Some of them want that, don't they?"

"They'll learn in much the same way as they always have. They'll pick up things from us—it's just that we won't be forcing it down their throats in quite the same way. And at least we'll be acknowledging the fact that we might just be wrong."

He wanted to gasp. Relativism took his breath away. Morality and aesthetics could be relative, but the laws of physics? Who in their right mind would question Bernoulli's principle when in an aircraft at thirty thousand feet?

"Wrong about microbiology?" he challenged. "Might we be wrong about that?"

"People have been wrong about scientific paradigms in the past," she retorted.

"Yes, but—"

"All I'm saying is that we might be less didactic," said Chrissie. "I think that's the message that Henrietta's trying to get across. She wants us to listen to the students. We're not here just to tell them what to do. They have their views."

"Possibly."

She pointed a finger at him. "Your trouble, you know, is that at heart you don't want anything to change. You're too dyed-in-the-wool."

He resented this. "That's not true," he countered, feeling the back of his neck becoming warm. They said that was a sure sign of conservatism, but he rejected such glib views. Anybody could feel hot at the back of their neck.

"Henrietta's a woman," said Chrissie, with the air of one explaining something obvious. "Bear in mind what she has had to do to get where she is today."

"Step on people?"

She gave him a dismissive look. "Women have to be seen to be tough. They have to make it clear that they are not going to be swayed by emotion. Can't you see that?"

"You're suggesting that they have to be as ruthless as men? That they have to be as *bad* as men?"

She took a moment to reply. "I admire her."

He was silent. Then, "Really?"

"Yes, I do."

He hesitated. "So you're on her side?"

"Not in everything. I'm just saying that you have to understand why she may have to do . . . certain things, I suppose, that might seem extreme to you. She has to. She's a politician."

He frowned. "A politician? I thought she was a scientist."

"Everybody in authority today is a politician," she shot back. "That's the way it is now. Everything is politicised."

He looked away. She might be right, but the thought depressed him, just as he was depressed by the thought of culture wars. There had been a Hundred Years' War in European history. Would the culture wars last that long? Possibly. He thought of the years of distrust and division that lay ahead—a prolongation of a cold war that stretched out into the future, touching all human feelings with its pervasive ice.

They lay in their bed that night, separated by sheets and, it seemed, by a gulf of ideology. She dropped off before he did, and he listened to her breathing becoming more regular as she slipped into the embrace of sleep. In the past, when they had a row, they had always apologised before they turned out the lights— a little rule they had. That had not happened now.

Neil did not consider himself an extremist of any stripe: he had always imagined that he was fairly and squarely in the middle of the political spectrum. He did not like the hard left, nor the selfish right. He believed in public goods and tolerance and helping the weak. He understood that people might have very different views of what was good, and that others should not be demonised simply because they disagreed with us. He did not think that patriarchal power was a good thing—societies in which it applied were, in his view, places of unhappiness, unfairness, and repression. But he did not feel that all authority should be questioned. Nor did he accept any of the concomitants of that position: the silencing, the censoring, the berating.

He turned in bed and looked at her sleeping form. What did he feel for her? He had liked her when they had first met. They had got on well. And they had become lovers because that was how things turned out if you were with somebody and you felt affectionate, and you took her hand, and one thing led to another. It was biology. But love was something rather more complicated than that. Had he ever loved her? He was not sure. He had felt tenderness. He had enjoyed her company. They had laughed together and taken pleasure in sharing. But he was worried that none of that amounted to love.

Love was something different. Love was an ache—an ache of the soul that was the authentic signature of love. It had happened to him before, and it was unmistakable. The first time had been at thirteen, and it had returned sporadically thereafter, like a recurring fever. That was why people talked about being lovesick; the metaphors of illness fitted so very well. And that feeling, he realised, never came from mere fondness, nor from friendship; it came from something quite distinct from other emotions.

And yet their relationship had something to it, and he imagined that it could develop into the love that he wanted. It had survived the occasional expression of puzzling and inexplicable views. Chrissie was unusual that way—she had certain fixed ideas, that came to the surface at odd times. She had once been dismissive of skiing. She thought that this was a risky and elitist sport that was environmentally degrading and should be discouraged. He had found it difficult to believe that somebody could take that view about something as innocent as sliding down hills on long narrow strips of . . . what were skis made of? Plastic? Wood? He had simply laughed at her views on that, and nothing more had been said. But what had passed between them this evening was more significant. This had all the makings of a real disagreement—one of a sort that could open up a gulf of difference.

Three

The casus belli arose innocently, unheralded, and might almost have blown over were it not for the particular tenacity of a young man called Tom Barnes. He had red hair and a deep sense of having been wronged when he was dropped—for extremism—from his high school debating team. That injustice, as he saw it—that example of the unaccountable exercise of educational authority, accompanied him from school to university, as a wrong that called out to be righted.

The world according to Tom was a place of fundamental unfairness. There was no point in trying to reform it through persuasion: those in authority were complicit in a whole groaning edifice of oppression that should only be met with determined resistance at every point. At least some people understood how he felt about the system, even if their understanding was incomplete, as he knew the understanding of others so often to be. There had been a sympathetic mathematics teacher, a mild, rather defeated man who habitually wore a crumpled corduroy jacket; his instincts, Tom felt, flowed in the right direction. This teacher said to him, "Yes, Tom, the world is exactly as you say it is. It's full of inequality and injustice. Anybody with any sense at all can see that. And you're right—we don't have to accept that. But you won't change it by charging at it head-on. You change it by putting things right one issue at a time, step by step."

"That's gradualism," Tom retorted. "And it's a waste of time. It gets you nowhere."

The teacher sighed. He had known countless seventeen-year-olds. Of course they thought that way: it was a result of the way their brains were wired; an appreciation of gradualism came only after years of witnessing the failure of quicker solutions. At seventeen, there was no room for nuance: conviction was everything. Yet he loved them for that: at least they believed in something with their *hearts*. That was something so precious, so vital. And yet . . . He sighed again. Sometimes there seemed to be no point in trying to get these young people to see things in another light, to broaden their perspective. But he had to make an attempt; that was his duty as a teacher. He had to. "Revolution can do the same, you know," he said mildly. "You don't end injustice by destroying everything in sight."

Tom looked at the teacher with pity. What did this man know about revolution? As a teacher he was part of the system, even if he, individually, was less remote than most of them.

By the time Tom enrolled at university, he had identified his target. There was an establishment—anywhere you looked, in any organisation or institution—dominated by people who had a strong interest in remaining where they were, and in holding onto such power as they had. This was glaringly obvious, he thought. Look around you: there it was, embodied in the people who ran things. He had to act, he felt, and the way in which he could do this would be to play whatever role he could in student politics. He might have some influence there—not much, perhaps, but at least he would be doing something, rather than simply observing. And for Tom, to be doing something was important: the injustice of the world hurt him in a real and immediate way; he could not understand how anybody could be indifferent to it—how anybody could live their lives as if that great sea of unhappiness that was the lot of so many people throughout the world simply did not exist. How could they?

There was a student council, and Tom was soon elected to it unopposed. His manifesto—a few short lines—stressed the need to redress what he called the marginalisation of the voiceless. Nobody was going to argue with him about that, and he set about pursuing this goal in his immediate surroundings. There were issues to address, and he tackled them one after another in turn. Every now and then, a major opportunity presented itself, and he was able to promote a small dispute into a significant and bitter row. His greatest achievement was to foment a twenty-four-hour student strike over plagiarism proceedings against a candidate for a master's degree. The candidate in question, he argued, had acted in good faith and had not understood that using unacknowledged material in an assignment was wrong. "Words can't be the property of just one person," he said. "Words belong to language—and language belongs to all of us."

Henrietta became aware of Tom after he had led the student strike. She invited him to her office, where she offered him coffee and a piece of Black Forest gateau. He looked at the cake with ill-concealed suspicion. He was not to be so easily bought off.

She noticed. "The cake has no strings attached," she said, with a smile. "I only invited you in to let you know that I fully understand the point you're making about this plagiarism business. The problem is that the disciplinary action taken against the student in question was initiated by another university official—not by me."

He gave her a searching look. "You had nothing to do with it?"

She shook her head. "Of course not. I believe the candidate, and I'm going to make sure that the matter is dropped by the university to which he is affiliated. They'll give him his degree."

Tom looked at the cake.

"So, please, enjoy the cake—if you like that sort of thing. Some people find Black Forest gateau a little rich."

He reached for the cake, and broke off a piece. It was crumbly and sticky at the same time.

"I think you'll find that you and I are on the same page on many matters," Henrietta continued. "And if there is anything you ever need to discuss with me, my door is always open. Please remember that."

He wiped the crumbs from his lips. "Okay."

"Good."

The institute provided teaching for two of the courses for which Tom Barnes had registered at one of the universities. One of these, the Control of Communicable Disease in Urban Conditions, was taught by Neil, along with a medical sociologist. The socio-economic issues were dealt with by the sociologist, while Neil covered the scientific side of the course. Much of that was practical and down to earth—a matter of drains, water purification, and the control of rats. "Our little enemy," Neil said, showing a slide of a rat, facing the lens, bright eyes reflecting back the camera's flash. "*Rattus rattus*, to give him his full name. Wanted since the fourteenth century for complicity in the spreading of the bubonic plague, but possibly not to blame for that after all. Still, he remains a vector for the spread of disease, as well as for the consumption of vast quantities of grain otherwise intended for human consumption."

A major threat of disease, though, came through human agency. "We do exactly the things we shouldn't do," Neil explained to his students. "We travel too much. We huddle together in close proximity. We live in overcrowded cities. It's small wonder that disease can spread rapidly."

Seated at the back of the lecture theatre, Tom watched and listened. He made a note on the pad in front of him; he played with his ballpoint pen, revealing and concealing its point. The young woman sitting next to him scowled at the clicking sound, but Tom was engaged elsewhere. He was paying attention to what Neil was saying about conditions in a shanty town on the outskirts of Rio de Janeiro. A study had recently been conducted of early mortality in tin-sided houses erected on the slopes of a hill. These were often occupied, Neil said, by two or three families. There was no running water available, other than from municipal standpipes; and pit latrines, standing cheek by jowl with the houses, were the only form of sanitation.

"Against this background," Neil continued, "the insanitary lifestyle of some of the occupants becomes even more of a public health issue."

Tom stiffened. He clicked his pen once more and wrote a few words on his notepad.

"And there are plenty of examples of similar insanitary lifestyles closer to home," Neil continued. "When I was working in public health in Glasgow, I was once called to a flat in Drumchapel. I saw dirty plates piled sky high around a sink that hadn't been cleaned since goodness knows when. I remember the cockroaches scuttling away when we went in. It was disgusting."

Tom made a few further notes. His brow was furrowed; it was obvious to the young woman sitting beside him that he was concerned over something. She gave him an enquiring glance.

"Bourgeois prig," muttered Tom under his breath.

She smiled. "You don't need to take it personally," she whispered. "He's not talking about you."

"He's talking about ordinary people," replied Tom. "Those people are victims. It's not their fault they live in those conditions. He called *them* disgusting. Did you hear that? He used the word *disgusting* to describe ordinary, working-class people."

"I think he meant that the conditions were disgusting—not the people."

Tom shook his head. "I heard him," he said. "He called *them* disgusting. That's what he said."

She shrugged. "Suit yourself."

At the end of the lecture, Tom went to Henrietta's office. She received him courteously. "I haven't any Black Forest gateau," she said. "Sorry. I'm meant to be on a diet and that stuff . . . well, it's not exactly low calorie."

Tom had not come to talk about Black Forest gateau. "I'd like to make a complaint," he said. "I'm not sure what the procedure is, but you did say that if I needed help on anything."

She looked at him over her half-moon glasses. "I did say that."

"Well, I want to make a complaint about one of the academic staff."

Her manner became cautious. "I see."

She waited.

"Dr. Neil Anderson."

She remained quite still. Then, quietly, she said, "Would you like to tell me about it?"

"He made a disparaging remark," Tom said.

"Oh, yes? About . . . about you?"

Tom told her that it had not been about anybody in the room. "It was about people living in difficult conditions. Ordinary people. He called them disgusting."

She continued to look at him over her glasses. He shifted in his seat. He was not entirely comfortable, but he was in the right, he thought. The remark had been made and he was entirely justified in bringing it to her attention. What was he expected to do? To tolerate that sort of thing?

Henrietta moved the papers in front of her. She would have to be careful.

"Could you tell me exactly what Dr. Anderson said?" she asked. "I need to know what his precise words were."

Tom hesitated. He looked slightly aggrieved. He had already told her. "Well, he said something about being in a flat in Drumchapel and seeing something. He said the people who lived there were disgusting."

Henrietta looked away. "He said these people were disgusting? That was the word he used: *disgusting*?"

Tom nodded. "I was pretty upset by that. Okay, Drumchapel is a challenging place, but you can't say that people living there are disgusting, can you?"

She shook her head. "Of course, you can't. Conditions in an area like that can be difficult—but that's not the fault of the people themselves."

"They have no chance in life," Tom said. "None. Bad housing. No jobs. What can they do?"

She sat back in her chair. "That was all Dr. Anderson said?"

Tom nodded. Surely that was enough.

Henrietta moved her papers again. "Would you put this in writing, please—that is, if you wish to make this an official complaint."

He bit his lip. The establishment may have a friendly face, but it could be entirely different underneath. Their procedures were designed to slow things down, to enmesh people in bureaucratic formalities. He asked, "Do I have to?"

"If you wish to make it official, yes."

He met her stare. "Do you think I should?"

Her answer came quickly. "Let's say, semi-official. I think it would be best, now that you've raised it with me."

He asked her what that involved, and she replied that it meant that the matter would be dealt with—"I hope to your satisfaction"—but that this would be done without recourse to procedures that could involve hearings. "The point is that sometimes people may have the law on their side, you see, and then . . ." She gave him a meaningful look. "And then we may not get what we want, if you see what I mean."

He noticed that she said *we*. You had to be careful; people who were really on the other side made you think that they were acting *with* you. He had read that somewhere, and he suspected it was true. You had to remember who *we* were.

He nodded, and told her that he would write her an email. Then he said, "I don't care if he knows I'm the one who's complained. You can tell him. I don't want to shelter behind anybody."

"All right," she said. "It's probably better that way. But we should still keep it relatively informal." As she spoke, she was deciding what to do. This whole allegation was too flimsy; it was not worth doing much about it. If it came to an official enquiry, it would rapidly become apparent that there was little or no reliable evidence. And, more importantly, it would be others who would be in control. If she kept it as her issue, she might be able to make something of it. She was aware that not all her new colleagues were behind her, and she thought that Neil was probably one of those who had been lukewarm about her appointment: he had that look about him. This was an opportunity to let him know who was in the driving seat: this would give her some leverage over him, which could be useful in the future. She would have a word with Neil and tell him to clarify what he meant and to apologise. And, as she looked at Tom sitting in front of her, she came to the realisation that she did not believe him. This young man was lying; she could tell. He was useful, yes, and he might prove an ally in the future, but on this particular matter it would be dangerous to trust him. Something had been said, but it was probably not what he was insisting it was.

She thought that, but what she said was, "I'm so sorry that you've been upset by these . . . by these unfortunate remarks. I think, on balance, that we should try to deal with this informally."

He said nothing. She noticed that his top lip was quivering. This gave her confidence.

"I should imagine that Dr. Anderson will be pleased to apologise," she continued. "He doesn't need to know who you are. He can issue an apology through me, and I shall pass it on to you. There could also be an apology to the whole class—that might be helpful, just in case there are other people in the room at the time who were offended but don't want to come forward." She paused. "Not everyone, you see, will be as public-spirited as you."

He considered this. He had done as much as he could for the time being. There would be other opportunities. "I suppose so," he said. This person was part of the system. He had decided. She was not going to admit it, but that was what she was.

Four

She waited just over an hour before calling Neil to invite him to her office.

"A small matter has cropped up," she said, her tone friendly, but with a hint of weariness. He should know that her job was not an easy one: sometimes people without administrative responsibilities failed to understand the pressures.

"A student matter," she added. "It needs attention."

He told her that he would be with her in ten minutes, and they rang off. He was puzzled, and wondered what the issue was. Some of his students were finding the course a bit onerous, he suspected, and he had heard that there were rumblings of discontent over the workload. It was probably that.

But when he went into Henrietta's office, he sensed immediately that it was something more serious. She greeted him in a rather remote way, indicating with a sharp movement of her hand that he should sit down. This was not going to be a fireside chat, he thought.

"I'm sorry to say," Henrietta began. "There has been a complaint about you."

Neil's surprise was clearly genuine. Henrietta saw that, and her immediate reaction was to soften. "Not a major one," she said quickly. "Nothing we can't sort out easily enough, but you know how these student issues can become a bit tricky if not dealt with tactfully."

He did not say anything.

"I'll come straight to the point," Henrietta said. "I've had a student in here, Tom Barnes—I tell you that in confidence—saying that you described people—members of the public—as disgusting. That was the word he said you used."

Neil stared at her. A smile of incredulity spread over his face. "Me?"

"Yes. He alleges that you said that in a lecture."

Neil shook his head. This was ridiculous. "Who?" he asked. "Who's disgusting? I mean, who am I meant to have said is disgusting?"

Henrietta realised just how little information she had. It was just as well that she had decided to avoid official channels.

"The student in question was a bit vague," she admitted. "He didn't spell it out—other than to say that you called them disgusting."

"But who's *them?*" insisted Neil.

"He said something about ordinary people."

"But *which* ordinary people." He shook his head again. "I really don't know what this student, whoever he or she is, is talking about." He paused briefly. "I wouldn't say that—I just wouldn't. I don't say that sort of thing about . . . about anyone."

Henrietta felt her advantage slipping away. Her tone became firmer. "He said that you did. He was quite specific. He said that you mentioned Drumchapel. He implied it was a class thing."

Neil's eyes widened. This was absurd. "A class thing?" He wanted to laugh.

She lowered her eyes. "He implied that you viewed ordinary, working-class people as disgusting."

Neil burst out laughing. "But that's what I am myself," he said. "Are we talking about self-hatred here? I'm an ordinary person. My origins are working class, if you want to put it that way. My father was a warehouseman. I went to a state school, in so far as that says anything. If I were to describe myself as anything, it would be as working class."

He looked at her. He felt tempted to ask Henrietta what her origins were. In his experience, people who went on about social class tended to come from more privileged backgrounds than his. Class was a middle-class obsession—not that it meant all that much any longer.

His response took her aback. It would have been far easier, she thought, if he came from a more vulnerable position—if he had been privately educated, for example, as she herself had been.

His astonishment had expressed itself in laughter and a smile. Now it changed. "I just wouldn't say anything like that," he repeated. "I wouldn't. I don't think that way—as I've told you."

She fiddled with her papers. "I'm not saying that you did. It's possible that the student in question misheard—"

"He must have," interjected Neil.

She did not like being interrupted. She raised her voice slightly. "Or misunderstood what you said. That's a possibility, I suppose."

"It's not a possibility," Neil said quietly. "It happened. That's what happened. Or he's making it up."

"But why would he do that?"

Neil shrugged. "Because people do. There's such a thing as a false accusation. People make them for all sorts of reasons. They take a personal dislike, and—"

Now it was her turn to interrupt. "Why would one of your students take a personal dislike to you?"

"You tell me." He paused. "Not everybody gets on. You must know that."

He had not intended his response to carry any implication, but it clearly did. And that was the way she interpreted it: he was suggesting that not all the staff approved of her. That was the construction she put upon what he said. She took a deep breath. "I think we need to try not to make this personal."

"But it is personal," Neil responded. "It's a personal complaint against me."

For a few moments Henrietta was silent. This was not going well. It was clear that Neil was going to resist, and that meant she would lose any chance that she had in playing this situation to her advantage. It could become messy, and the university authorities might blame her for the fact that an embarrassing situation—possibly even one that could end up in the press—should have arisen on her watch. She would need to avoid that at all costs.

Her tone became conciliatory. "What I suggest is this," she began. "I think you should issue an apology for using words that inadvertently—and I stress, inadvertently—caused offence. We will then say—we, as an institute, of course—that our policy on this is very clear: no student should feel threatened in any of our courses. Everybody is safe. That's our position."

He stared at her, struggling to control himself. He wanted to shout. But when he spoke, it was in a quiet, firm tone. "No," he said. "I don't see why I should apologise for something I didn't do."

She folded her hands. She was Portia, proposing a solution, and it was unwise of him not to see that.

"I think you should think about it very carefully. I think you should go off and consider the various options. Do you want a full-scale row? Or do you want to put the whole thing to bed and continue with your work? A simple apology—along the lines I've suggested—would mean the whole thing would quickly be forgotten. There would be no casualties."

"Except truth," Neil said quickly.

She closed her eyes. He was trying her patience. She had pro-

posed an easy solution and this foolish man was perversely not seeing it as the easy way out that it was.

"Just think about it," she repeated. "Let's talk about it tomorrow . . ." She glanced at the diary that lay open on her desk. "No,
I'm in meetings all day tomorrow, and then I'm off to London for a
couple of days. A conference. Let's say next week. Let's meet and
talk about it then."

He rose to his feet. "I'm not going to apologise for something I
haven't done."

She looked away, avoiding his gaze. "Next week," she said. "Let
me know in due course what time would suit you. My door is always
open."

That evening it was Neil's turn to cook dinner, as Chrissie
went to a Pilates class after work. On occasion, she brought one of
her fellow members back with her, for a meal in the flat, but this did
not happen this time. She went directly to shower, and by the time
she made her way into the kitchen, their meal of salmon steaks and
broccoli was ready to serve. Neil had poured her a glass of chilled
white wine, and had lit a candle on the table. The candle was a cus-
tom that had grown up between them; it was always one of the green
Swedish candles that she bought from a Scandinavian decor shop
not far from the institute.

She asked about his day.

"Not good," he replied, lifting the salmon from the pan.

She sat down and took a sip of her wine. She assumed that he was
referring to work: he was halfway through a project that had run
into unexpected difficulties. It was questionable whether any of the
data would be usable and it might be necessary for the whole thing
to be started afresh.

"I had a bad feeling about that," she said. "That postgrad you took on seemed a bit flaky to me. I'm not surprised that—"

He stopped her. "Not that."

"Something else?"

He put a large knob of butter on top of the broccoli. "Not too much," she cautioned. "I don't want to undo the good of my Pilates."

He passed her a plate. "I saw Henrietta today."

She took another sip of wine. "Oh, yes? I saw her this afternoon. She was telling me that she's off to a conference. Cambridge, I think."

He corrected her. "London. The London School of Hygiene and Tropical Medicine. Alastair's unit." Alastair was a friend of his from school days—a high-flying infectious tropical medicine physician who specialised in the transmission of malaria. "They're working with those people in Oxford. He thinks they might—just might—be getting close to a malaria vaccine."

"I heard that. I hope that guy in Oxford has space on his wall for the Nobel citation."

He sat down. "We didn't talk about any of that," he said. "There's been a complaint."

"Students?" she asked. "They're always complaining."

"There's a student called Tom—"

She looked up. "Barnes? The one with red hair?"

He nodded. "Yes. Him. He's complained."

"He looks about fifteen, that guy," she said. "I picture him sitting in his room playing his PlayStation."

"Well, he's found the time and energy to complain. He's something in a student association somewhere."

"Complaints officer, perhaps."

He tried to smile. "Actually, it's about me."

She put down her knife and fork. "About you? Giving them too many assignments? Expecting them actually to do the reading?"

He shook his head. "He's accusing me of saying something offensive."

She sat back in her chair. "I don't believe it," she said. Then, "What precisely?"

"He says that I called the entire population of Drumchapel disgusting—something like that."

She burst out laughing. "Drumchapel? Over in Glasgow?"

"Yes. He said that I made disparaging references to their lifestyle."

She threw up her hands. "But what else can you say? That's one of the epicentres of the bad Scottish diet. It's a disaster. And everyone smokes and drinks. Look at the high mortality figures— I bet Drumchapel's right up there."

"I know that. But he said that it was a sort of dismissive, arrogant remark about working-class people there. He accused me, I suppose, of writing them off."

Now she exploded. "But that's ridiculous. You're not like that."

"Thanks. I'd never make a remark like that. I disapprove of some aspects of the lifestyle—sure. Drinking to excess. Smoking. All of that. But I know full well that the people over there are up against it. Poverty. Unemployment. You name it. If anything, I sympathise with them. I know how hard it is to get out of all that."

"Of course you do."

He shook his head in exasperation. "We tell people to eat a healthy diet, but then we forget what a healthy diet costs. It's out of reach to a lot of people. Junk food's cheaper." He paused. "I feel awful about this. Really awful."

She reached out to touch him. "You've got nothing to beat yourself up over. Nothing. That red-haired boy has got problems. Not you. You're not the one with a problem here."

He smiled at her. "At least you believe me."

She looked surprised. "You mean, Henrietta didn't?"

He explained that he found it difficult to work out what Henrietta felt. "She plays her cards close to her chest. She's that type. But I had the feeling that she wasn't on my side."

Chrissie sat back in her chair. "Are you sure? She might just have been . . . how might one put it? Just being formal. I suppose that somebody in her position has to *appear* impartial."

"But who's to believe that sort of thing? She may not know me all that well, but she should realise that I wouldn't be doing what I do if I thought that way." He shrugged. Henrietta would never be interested in what he thought about things—he was well aware of that. She was indifferent to him, at best. For a few moments he felt something close to self-pity—the feeling of those who know that they are misjudged by one who has not bothered to find out what they think or do. "You don't go into public health if you think like that about the people you're meant to be looking after. It doesn't make sense."

Even as he said this, he realised that it made him sound self-righteous. To forfend that, he went on, "There are plenty of people more committed than I am. I'm not saying I'm anything special."

"Of course you're not." She made a gesture that conveyed a certain helplessness. There was a zeitgeist to be considered. She sighed. "You know what things are like these days."

He waited for her to say more.

"People are scared," she continued. "They worry about being publicly attacked. Accused of this or that. People are terrified of being hounded for saying the wrong thing, even inadvertently."

He looked at her. She was right. There was every reason for fear. They lived in intolerant times, in which subtleties were eclipsed by the comfort of certainty.

"Sometimes," he said, "I think that we're back where we were in the . . . what was it? The seventeenth century. We burned witches in Scotland then. And heretics. We still have witch-hunts, I suppose. They're not called that, but that's what they can be."

She frowned. "Yes, I suppose so."

"People are always ready to turn on one another, I think. They want somebody to blame. They want to punish somebody for . . ." He looked at her, and wondered whether she was interested in all this. They did not talk about these things very much, if at all, and he had assumed that she saw the world in roughly the same light as he did. Most couples did that, he imagined. And yet now it occurred to him that there might be a real difference between the values they espoused.

Yet she nodded at his analogy. She agreed. "It's awful. But yes, you're right. There still are witch-hunts. Think of those social media feeding frenzies."

He said, "I don't want to be burned at the stake."

They both laughed.

He poured himself a glass of wine. "I think Henrietta might make quite a credible Witchfinder General, don't you? She has the nose for it."

She hesitated. "She might not be as bad as you think she is."

He frowned at the sympathy, and yet there must be people who saw her in a positive light: we all have someone who thinks the world of us. He found it hard to warm to Henrietta, but perhaps he was being harsh: Neil was not vindictive. "Are you sure you're not being too kind?"

"No, I'm just trying to be fair. She can be a bit—"

"Calculating?"

"Maybe. But she does her best, I think."

This was going a bit far for Neil. "Does her best for whom? For herself?"

She gave him a reproachful look, and he realised that he must have sounded uncharitable. There must be good points there— if one looked for them. Presumably Henrietta believed in the work they were doing and wanted it to succeed. And she must have the interests of the students at heart. He wanted to believe that, and for a few moments he did. Perhaps she felt protective towards Tom Barnes; it was possible that she saw him as callow and vulnerable. Perhaps she was simply showing kindness, which, after all, people did, although sometimes we had to remind ourselves of that fact. It was easy to become cynical about the motives of others, and to assume that self-interest was more powerful than it really was.

They lapsed into silence, broken, at last, when Chrissie asked what would happen next.

"Henrietta said that we should talk after she comes back from London. She says that she wants to sort it out informally—whatever that means."

Chrissie looked thoughtful. "It might have blown over by then."

"Do you think so?" he asked.

She hesitated before answering him. "No, not really." She relented, though, for the bleak response. Now she said, "I've got a feeling this isn't going to last. This boy, this Tom character, might find a girlfriend. That'll help."

He grinned. "Do you really think sexual frustration lies at the heart of—"

She did not let him finish. "Everything? At the heart of everything?" She paused. "No, not everything. Some things, perhaps, but not everything."

She raised her glass and looked through it—through the meniscus of wine. "His problem is his red hair," she said—and laughed.

He thought: I don't find it funny.

She picked that up, and said, "You don't need to worry about this—you really don't. These things come and go."

He thought: but I'm the victim of a false accusation—you aren't. You can make light of it, but I can't.

Five

Over the days that followed, Neil tried to put the complaint out of his mind. He succeeded, at least initially, as he was busy at work. He had a report to write—a lengthy document that was proving slow to emerge from a morass of data—and it occupied most of his waking hours. This took his attention off the course he was running, although he knew that he had a lecture to deliver, and that he would find himself standing once again before his accuser. When that occasion eventually arose, he noticed Tom sitting towards the back of the lecture theatre. He was just a boy, he thought: a nineteen-year-old, or whatever he was, with comparatively little experience of the world, and his heart fixed prominently on his sleeve. Thinking of him in those terms made it almost possible to feel a certain fondness for him. Who amongst us, he thought, was not an idealist at that age? When you were nineteen you were still technically in your teens, and should be forgiven everything—for just about everything. Of course, people at Tom's stage wanted to change the world, and if that involved exposing attitudes they found unacceptable, then that became more than an option—it became an obligation. Tom was simply doing his duty. The ability to exercise judgement came later—sometimes much later—and that was the point at which we became accountable for any damage our zeal might cause.

He saw that beside him was a young woman wearing an odd, pastel-coloured jumper. She had around her neck a light silk scarf tied in a loose knot; he could see from her expression that she was amused by something. As he delivered the lecture, she leaned towards Tom from time to time and whispered in his ear. Tom acknowledged her comments with a slight movement of his head; on one occasion he smiled in response to something she said to him. Neil thought there was an intimacy about them—this, perhaps, was the girlfriend that Chrissie had prescribed for him, but he was not sure; she did not seem to be taking notes, and he decided it likely that she was not enrolled for the course. Her face seemed vaguely familiar, but he could not remember where he had seen her, if indeed he had.

He tried not to look in Tom's direction, but that was difficult. The eyes have a habit of wandering in an unwanted direction, and when he glanced up from his notes, he found himself staring in his direction. Fortunately, Tom seemed to be absorbed by his notepad, or, on one or two occasions, by the young woman beside him. At the end of the lecture, Neil left hurriedly, and already was out of the door by the time the students spilled out into the corridor. Neil walked back to his office as swiftly as he could. As he closed his office door behind him, he saw the winking red light on his telephone that told him of a missed call. He sat down and pressed the button that would reveal his voicemail.

It was Henrietta. She sounded cheerful—almost breezy—and apologised for taking up his time. "I know you're very busy," the recording said, "but it would be most helpful if you could come round to my office for a quick word. I shall be here until six this evening, and any time will suit, but if you can manage more or less now, that would be helpful." There was a slight pause, followed by a courteous expression of thanks. The message then ended with an apology for taking up his time. "I know you have better things to do—and we all do, really—but I think we should get this matter sorted out as soon as possible. I'm sure you feel the same."

For a few moments he did nothing, and simply stared up at the ceiling. He realised that his heart was beating faster than normal, and he remembered what he had learned in his physiology class in those very early days of medical school. Fear or excessive excitement prompted the brain to release adrenaline, and this made the heart speed up. It was the fight-or-flight reaction, and he felt it now. He remembered, too, that the liver and pancreas were affected by the adrenaline surge. That was what was happening to him now. He closed his eyes and took a deep breath: the heart was not entirely beyond our control. The mind was master in its own house. He felt his heart slow down. He opened his eyes.

Henrietta had told her secretary to expect him, and so he was nodded into the office.

"You wanted to see me."

She stood up when he entered, and indicated for him to be seated.

"Thank you for coming so quickly."

He lowered himself into the chair before her desk. "How was the conference?"

"Ah, that. The London School of Hygiene and Tropical Medicine—I've always thought the title a real mouthful. And I must admit, I don't like the reference to hygiene. I find that a bit condescending."

He suppressed a smile. She would be embarrassed by the concept of hygiene. Henrietta would never presume to tell anybody to wash their hands.

"Oh, I don't know," he said. "It tells you what you're going to get in the tin. Hygiene's just an old-fashioned word for public health."

She nodded. "I suppose that's true. Do you know the school?"

He told her that he had been to several courses there, but they had been short ones. He had applied for a job there once and had been turned down. "I wasn't good enough."

She raised a hand. "No, you mustn't say that. Jobs there will attract scores of applications. There were probably several people who just had much more experience than you."

"That amounts to the same thing, though. They would have been better than me."

"You're being very modest," she said.

"Realistic, rather." He paused. They were still in the stage of pleasantries. He thought: she can be pleasant if she wants to be. This, presumably, was the side that the appointment committee had seen when they gave her the directorship. "And the conference?"

"It was mostly a survey of what was happening in various fields. There was quite a bit about bilharzia. Schistosomiasis. They had several people over from Cambodia, talking about *Schistosoma mekongi*. There are places there where it was endemic."

"Was?"

"The baseline infection rate in some areas used to be roughly eighty per cent." She paused for emphasis. "Can you believe it? Eighty per cent of the population."

"Well, it's waterborne, and people can't really avoid water, can they?"

She agreed. "The government opted for mass treatment of the whole population. They gave everybody in the affected areas hefty doses of praziquantel over a period of eight years."

He raised an eyebrow. "That's a lot of pills."

"Apparently, it worked. The incidence went right down. Through the floor, in fact."

"Nice result."

"There were no deaths from chronic long-term infection. And they added a dose of mebendazole while they were about it. That knocked helminth infections on the head. There was a real reduction in ringworm infection. Everybody was very pleased."

"Interesting."

He watched her. They would have to get to the point of the meeting—perhaps Henrietta wanted to put that off with this scientific exchange.

"Bilharzia is a fairly neglected disease," she continued. "It's just below malaria in terms of its impact in Africa and Asia—but nobody pays much attention to it. The people down in London became quite animated about that. They said that the degree of attention a disease received was directly dependent on the infection rate in wealthy populations. That's why research into dementia drugs is so well funded."

"A billion dollars a throw, I believe."

She sighed. "And then they fail. Everybody's hopes are up, and the results come in: no appreciable benefit. Back to the drawing board."

He looked at her. "You wanted to talk about the complaint."

It was as if she had not expected this. "Oh yes, the complaint. That."

He waited. She had spoken casually, almost dismissively, and for a moment he wondered whether she had abandoned any thought of taking the matter further. He felt a certain relief at that: he was satisfied of his innocence, but any complaint against you, even one without foundation—as this one so obviously was—was discomforting. If Henrietta had decided to take matters no further, he might even reconsider his attitude towards her. Perhaps she was not the ambitious bureaucrat he had imagined, but somebody who, behind an unpromising façade, had a capacity for sympathy. It was important not to misjudge people: everyone deserved a chance.

But he was not to get off that lightly.

"I gave the matter some thought while I was away," Henrietta said. "And I imagine that you've been thinking about it too."

She seemed to be expecting a response, and so he said, "On and off."

"And I've reached a view," Henrietta continued. "I think the simplest thing would be for you to apologise to the whole class. You don't have to address the student who raised the complaint—just say that you have become aware that something you said was perhaps a little bit insensitive. Say that you are now aware that your words could cause distress, and that you won't be speaking in those terms again. For my part, I'll speak to the complainant and give him a very clear steer to regard this apology as bringing the matter to an end. I have every confidence he'll accept your apology."

Neil sat quite still. There was a faint buzzing sound in his ears. Tinnitus, he thought; tinnitus brought about by a sudden increase in blood pressure. It took him a moment or two to collect his thoughts. He was expected to apologise—publicly.

"Let me get this straight," he said at last. "You want me to apologise for something I didn't say. Have I understood you correctly?"

Henrietta sighed, as if wearied by a deliberate failure on his part to understand something that was perfectly obvious. "It is true that I want you to apologise," she said. "But I would not say that you are being asked to apologise for something you didn't do."

It was clear enough to Neil. "I won't, I'm afraid. I am not going to apologise for a comment that I not only did not make, but that I wouldn't dream of making anyway." He paused, then added, "Sorry, but I am not going to acquiesce in this particular piece of Stalinism."

Henrietta recoiled. "Stalinism? Are you seriously suggesting that my solution—the peaceful compromise I've proposed—is Stalinist?"

He bit his lip. "No, all I want to say is that this is utterly unfair. It's more than that—it's ridiculous."

The mention of Stalinism had riled Henrietta, whose tone was now icily distant.

"It's very easy," she said, "to level accusations against people who are simply trying to broker a compromise."

He did not know what to say. Why should there be a compromise with a complete falsehood? Because that was what the accusation against him was. Compromise implied that there were two defensible, or at least understandable, positions to be taken into account. It was not like that here—one side here was in error; it was completely without merit. He had simply not said what he was accused of saying. That was all there was to it.

"So," she said, "you are not prepared to rebuild bridges?"

He hesitated. This was outrageous. He had done nothing to destroy any bridges—nothing at all. Eventually he said, "I don't see how I can do that without accepting something which is completely untrue." He slowed down. "Let me repeat: I did not say what I am accused of saying. I did not. Can I be any clearer?"

She looked away. She would not meet his gaze, and at that moment he despised her for her lack of courage.

"You make yourself perfectly clear," she said, still not looking at him.

Look at me, he thought. *Look at me.*

She did, but, rather, she looked *through* him. "That's your considered position?"

He nodded. "Considered? Yes." And added, "What alternative do I have—other than capitulation to a groundless accusation?"

She sat back in her chair. "In that case, I shall have to take the matter further and report the matter to the administration." She paused. "Of course, they may establish that what you are telling me is, in fact, the truth. But at least we shall have gone through the process."

He was undeterred by that. Perhaps it would be better to subject the whole ridiculous thing to formal examination. That would lead to his vindication—he was sure of that—even if it would be an uncomfortable experience.

"You understand what I'm saying," said Henrietta.

"Of course."

"And I'm afraid you'll be suspended until that process has been resolved—one way or another."

He opened his mouth, but no words came.

"On full pay, of course," Henrietta went on. "And you may continue, naturally, to carry out your research—privately. But you must not teach any courses during the suspension period, nor make any statement to the press, should they ask for one. Do you understand that?"

He nodded mutely. He was too shocked to do much else.

"I wish it could have been otherwise, Neil," said Henrietta. "I think that you're being unnecessarily stubborn."

Neil recovered. He did not have to lie down and put up with this. He was a senior lecturer; he was a member of the Faculty of Public Health and the Royal College of Physicians of Edinburgh. He did not have to accept being spoken to as if he were an errant twelve-year-old. "I'm being stubborn," he asked, "because I'm not prepared to apologise for something I didn't say?"

She waved a hand airily. "All I would say is that you're being stubborn. You're not co-operating."

"May I engage a lawyer?" Neil asked. "Would that help?"

There was irony in his tone, but Henrietta missed it. "If you wish," she replied. "In fact, that's probably quite a good idea."

He stood up to leave. He wanted to shout at her. He wanted somehow to prick the bubble of self-righteousness in which she seemed permanently to sit. "And who will teach my courses?" he asked.

Henrietta smiled. "There are any number of people who would jump at your job."

"Or yours," muttered Neil, his voice barely above a whisper.

She heard him. "Is that a threat?" she asked.

"An observation," said Neil.

The tension in the air had been building up like an electric charge. But now Henrietta seemed to relax. "I think we need a bit of time to cool down," she said. "Let's meet again at the end of the week. I have to be at a conference over the next few days. Seville."

"Another conference?" said Neil. "Seville? Very nice."

She gave him a cold look. "Conferences are work," she said. "Please don't imagine that I seek them out."

What she said was untrue, and he was about to snap back with a reply, but restrained himself. He knew that a sizeable number of conference invitations came to the institute's office, and were not directed towards specific people. Henrietta might have given colleagues a chance to attend, but many of the invitations never got past her desk—or so Neil had heard.

He asked, "I take it I'm still suspended?"

"Yes," she said. "Suspended from teaching—that's all. And informally—at the moment. Nobody is asking you to leave the premises." She grinned. "Your suspension—even if it's informal— is still a public statement. Surely you can see that."

He stared at her. "Why?"

"Why what?"

"Why is it a public statement? And intended for whom?"

She answered without delay. "For the people who feel aggrieved."

His eyes widened. "People? Plural? So there's more than one complainant?"

She looked flustered. "Not necessarily. But I think it safe to assume that if one student was upset there will be others."

The people who feel aggrieved . . . One thing was certain in his mind: these people were not the people who lived in Drumchapel, the people whose domestic conditions were so bleak. They were not the ones who were up in arms—it was a young man in Edinburgh who came, for all he knew, from a comfortable, if not privileged, background, and who had probably never seen the conditions to which he had referred in his lecture. He himself had worked with that; he had experienced it, and all he had said was that he found domestic squalor disgusting. And it was—it just was. That said nothing—implied no judgement—as to the cause of the squalor. That was a much bigger story—and it had its roots in deprivation and injustice over long years. And ignorance, too, although ignorance was rarely the fault of the ignorant. He knew all that, and the knowledge made him angry too. People should not have to live in poverty if the means existed to bring poverty to an end. That was often difficult, but you had at least to try to ameliorate the suffering that poverty entailed.

He closed his eyes. This was mob justice—or, rather, mob injustice. Of course, it was nothing particularly unusual—innocent people must suffer all the time under our imperfect human institutions. There were, he imagined, innocent people in prison even as they sat there. The system, with all its rules and procedures, was designed to prevent such outcomes, but there must be cases where it failed to do that. He could imagine the horror of being at the receiving end of a miscarriage of justice. The pain must be unbearable; the sense of outrage overwhelming. And what would make it worse would be the knowledge that people—friends and family included—might not believe in one's innocence.

"Thank you."

He opened his eyes. She was thanking him, but for what?

"Thank you for coming to see me. Now, if you'll allow me, I must get on."

He rose to his feet.

"I'll make the arrangements for the teaching," she said. "When is your next class?"

He answered automatically. "It's next week. Tuesday."

She made a note. "I'm sorry for all this unpleasantness," she said slowly. "I wouldn't have wished it to develop this way."

He turned away. For the first time, he thought about resignation. He could always resign. It would take a few minutes to write the letter and deliver it to her, across her desk. He could leave. He could go back to clinical practice; he could simply walk out of this Orwellian nightmare and return to the rational world in which people got by without posturing and recrimination; a world in which people tolerated and approved of one another, instead of demonising those with whom they might disagree; a world that allowed for private thoughts and a lack of zeal.

He almost did that. He almost turned and uttered the words— *I resign*—that would bring this to an end. But he did not. I have no reason to, he said to himself—and to do so would be, in a very real sense, a betrayal of something worth defending. It would be a betrayal of truth. I have done nothing for which I should reproach myself, he told himself. A resignation would be a defeat, and a defeat for him would be a victory for Henrietta, a confirmation of her intention to impose her will on those with whom she worked. That was her goal, and if she had to pander to the enthusiasms of the moment, then that was what she would do. She did not care about justice—of course she did not; what concerned her was to be on the side of those who could protest most stridently. In this case, that was Tom Barnes, and any other student who might claim to have been offended or made to feel insecure. It was as simple as that: Henrietta sensed which way the wind was blowing and she would bend as required.

He paused at the door. He was nervous, and he felt his heart beating hard within him. He turned back to face Henrietta. She was staring at him, uncertain whether this encounter was going to be prolonged.

He did not think about it for any length of time, and his words were, as a result, not carefully chosen. They were, in fact, the first words that came into his head.

"Do you have a view on freedom of speech?" he asked.

She blinked—and he wondered for a moment if she understood the question. But she did, and after a few moments she answered, "Of course I believe in freedom of speech." There was a brief pause before she continued, "But there are limits to freedom. You know that as well as I do."

"Of course."

He was going to say more, but she continued, her voice slightly raised. "Freedom of speech," she said, "doesn't include the right to make others feel uncomfortable. At least, not in my book."

He struggled to contain himself. "But we're all going to feel some degree of discomfort—because there are things that are wrong with the world, and these things are going to challenge us. The result is an inevitable level of queasiness—which we can't wish out of existence, I'm afraid."

He noticed that she frowned as he made this point, and it occurred to him that Henrietta might be having difficulty in grasping his argument. He waited for her to say something, but she remained silent. It was clear to him from her expression that their brief and unsatisfactory encounter was over.

"All right," he muttered as he left the office.

He thought he heard her say, "What does that mean?" but he was not sure, and he was not going to prolong the meeting. Outside, in the corridor, he saw the young woman who had been sitting next to Tom in the lecture room. She glanced at him briefly, and then looked away, avoiding his gaze. Her body followed, as if to put more space between them.

He wanted to say to her, "I don't have leprosy," but he realised that would be futile. She would not take the reference; she might not even know what leprosy was. She belonged to a generation that knew so little and so much at the same time. When they were knowledgeable, they were very knowledgeable, but when they were ignorant, as he suspected she might be, then their ignorance tended to be profound.

S i x

He played squash with his friend James. They had been contemporaries at medical school, but on graduation their careers had diverged. James trained as dermatologist and had spent two years with Médecins Sans Frontières in Rwanda. On his return to Scotland, he had taken a job in a hospital in the Borders, although he still lived in Edinburgh for most of the week. He was a strong squash player—considerably better than Neil—but their games were always friendly, and Neil suspected that when he won, which was infrequently, it was only because James let him do so.

"You don't have to," he assured him. "I'm a good loser."

"Then be a good winner."

Neil laughed. "That's hard—when you know you don't deserve to win."

After each game, they crossed the road to the pub on the corner, where they shared a drink together.

James was gay. Neil had known about that even before his friend, after a great deal of hesitation, had come out. James had asked him whether he already knew.

"Of course," said Neil. "From the beginning. From the day we met, I suppose—that first day of medical school."

James was taken aback. "Really? You're not just saying that because you know now? It's not that, is it?"

Neil was apologetic. He sensed his friend's dismay, and he realised that he should not have said what he had said. "Put it this way—I knew and didn't know at the same time—if you get my meaning."

James looked crestfallen. "I didn't think you knew. But you suspected."

Neil was gentle. "Yes, I suspected. That was all: I didn't actually know." He paused. "Does it matter what people think—or thought?"

James looked at him as if he were missing something very obvious. "We all have illusions about how other people think about us." He paused. "Sometimes we don't want other people to know everything. And there may be reasons for that, don't you think?"

Neil nodded. He understood. That was why we let people get away with their illusions: it was a question of tact—or of kindness.

Now, after their game of squash, they were in the pub. It was a ritual with them—a brisk game of squash followed by an hour of conversation over a cold beer.

"We go back a long way, don't we?" Neil said.

"Into the mists of time," said James.

"So you don't mind my telling you what's going on in my life?"

"Why should I? I tell you, so why shouldn't you tell me." James's face clouded. "Issues with Chrissie?"

Neil shook his head. "No, not that."

James seemed relieved. "That's good. I wouldn't be the best adviser there." He grinned. "Not that you'll be surprised by that admission."

"Women are the same as men," said Neil. "Just a bit nicer."

James paused. "I'm not the greatest expert on women, of course."

"You have plenty of female friends, though. Even if they're platonic." That was true. James was popular with women, some of whom had confessed their regret at his unavailability.

"I do, yes. But they're just friends. There's a difference, isn't there?"

"Which means you'll never complicate those particular friendships." said Neil. "You're lucky."

They lapsed into silence. Then James said, "If it's nothing to do with Chrissie, then what is it? Financial?" He stopped himself, and looked at Neil with concern. "You're not ill, are you?"

"No. Not as far as I know."

James winced. "You know, that's what's always bothered me—the fact that one might be developing something and not know about it for years. And then suddenly it's a Stage 4 diagnosis and nobody knew it was there all the time. We've all seen patients in that position."

Neil took a deep breath. "I've been suspended," he said. "As from this morning. A student complaint."

James's eyes widened. "Something you said . . ." He hesitated; then, "Or something you've done?"

"I've done nothing," said Neil.

"Good. At least it's not . . ." He left the sentence hanging in the air.

Neil told him, and when the account of his conversations with Henrietta was finished, James shook his head in disbelief. "That doesn't surprise me," he said.

"You know her?"

James nodded. "We were on a committee together a couple of years ago. She disapproved of me—I could tell."

"Why would she disapprove of you?" asked Neil.

James smiled. "The obvious reason. I mean, look at me. What a disappointment I must be for some people. Anyway, what are you going to do? Get a lawyer? Take her to court?"

"There's going to be an enquiry or something of that nature."

James whistled. "Guilty as charged," he said. "The whole point about enquiries is to ratify what those in charge have already decided. I'm very sceptical about enquiries: I always have been."

Neil sighed. "I don't know what to do. One part of me wants to stand up to her, because it's just so unfair, so completely unfounded. The other wants to walk away."

James looked concerned. "You'd give up the job? Just like that?"

"Yes."

James shook his head. "You can't do that."

"Why not? There are plenty of other things I could do."

"You mean, in medicine?"

Neil hesitated. He had never thought of doing anything else, but it was always possible. A medical friend had recently started retraining as an accountant. He preferred figures to people, he said, half jokingly, but only half. That conversation had troubled Neil: was his own commitment to medicine as firm as he had thought it was? Was he doing what he did *out of habit*, which was, perhaps, how a surprisingly large number of people led their lives?

"I might just take a break. I could use the time to think about what to do next."

James looked doubtful. "You aren't the type to sit around." He looked away; his inherent distaste for disapproval made this hard for him—yet this was bullying, he thought, and it had to be confronted. "That woman doesn't deserve to be where she is."

Neil said that he thought the world was full of people who did not deserve to be where they were—and that particularly applied to people in positions of authority.

James agreed—to an extent. "Sometimes you come across somebody who deserves to be where they are—unambitious types who believe in the public good and want to do the right thing." He paused. "I don't think this applies to her—from what you tell me."

"I don't think so too."

James became resolute. "Resist," he said. "Stand up to them."

"I'm not sure—"

"You have to," he said. "It'll happen to others—until people stand up to them."

"Who's them, by the way?"

James made a despairing gesture. "The people who used to run inquisitions. The people who burned others at the stake—right here in Scotland. They haven't gone away, you know. They're still with us, although they have different causes. People who intimidate other people. People who set themselves up as guardians of public morality, and then behave like tyrants. Nobody's changed, you know."

Neil was silent.

James gave him a pleading look. "I know it's hard, but you have to do it. You have to say no to Henrietta and this student friend of hers." He paused. "You have to, Neil."

He went home. Chrissie was in the kitchen, preparing a meal. Neil had said that morning that he would cook dinner, but she had already started to make a moussaka.

"I was in the mood," she said. "I was going to do some reading, but I couldn't concentrate."

He went up to her and kissed her lightly on the cheek. He was happy to be with her. She touched him lightly on his arm—a gesture that he always found comforting. It was her way of saying to him that he had nothing to worry about: that she understood. He imagined that all couples had their little gestures of sympathy, familiar tics of affection that reassured the other that whatever happened, neither was alone.

She gave him a searching look. "Anything?"

He knew what she was talking about. He told her about his meeting with Henrietta.

As he spoke, she reached out and took his hand. He thought: I am like a child being comforted after a fight in the playground.

"That's bad," she said when he finished. "It looks like she has an agenda."

He considered this. It was probably true: Henrietta was not on his side. Did that mean, though, that there was personal animosity—or was it that he just happened to be in the wrong place? He could not decide: he had not previously felt that she disliked him; at least he had not thought that until now. He was, he imagined, an obstruction in her path—whatever her path was—he was not entirely sure of that, of course, but it was clear that he was somehow in the way.

He said, "Let's not talk about it. I'm fed up."

"I don't blame you," she replied. A frown crossed her brow. "But you can't bury your head in the sand, Neil."

He denied that he was doing this, but his denial sounded hollow—even to himself. Chrissie seemed to sense this, and she persisted. "You need to stick to your guns. Refuse to apologise—just refuse point-blank. You're in the right, after all."

He closed his eyes. "You're the second person to tell me that." He added, "The second person today."

"The other being?" she pressed.

"James."

She seemed pleased to hear this. "Well, there you are. James knows you. He's saying exactly what I'm saying. You have to stand your ground."

He sat down at the kitchen table. "So everyone seems to be saying."

"Well, everyone is right. Just refuse. She can't make you apologise—especially for something you didn't do."

He pointed out that Henrietta seemed to feel that she could do exactly that.

"Well," snapped Chrissie. "She's wrong."

"If I defy her," Neil said. "What then? If you refuse to follow an instruction from your head of department, can't you be fired?"

Chrissie frowned. "I doubt it. You have a contract. You're not casual labour."

But Neil was not so sure. "If you don't do what you're asked to do, aren't you in breach of that contract? Couldn't they argue that? Otherwise, what sanctions would any management have? None that I can see."

She was robust in her dismissal of his concern. "There's the small matter of employment law," she said. "You can go to a tribunal if you're unfairly dismissed. People can't be got rid of that easily—not these days. And rightly so."

"But would dismissal be unfair if you refuse to do what you're asked to do?"

Chrissie made a careless gesture. "You'd be fine," she said. "She can't dismiss you for refusing to do something she had no right to ask you to do."

He was not sure that he agreed, but he did not say anything.

"Tell her tomorrow," said Chrissie. "Tell her that you have nothing to apologise for. Tell her that they can suspend you all they like, but it'll make no difference."

He closed his eyes. He suddenly felt weary. He did not want to talk about this any longer.

"What did you do today? Anything?"

"Nothing happened at work—just the usual. But I had a tutorial this evening—online."

He smiled. "Your interior decoration course?"

"Yes. We've been doing colour co-ordination. We go on to fabrics next week. That's a whole module."

He nodded. "With the same tutor? What's his name?"

"Yes. Brian."

Neil asked if he was any good.

"Amazing. He's got a terrific eye."

"I suppose that's what you need. Do you like him?"

She turned away. He waited for an answer. It occurred to him suddenly: nobody will any longer say what they think.

"He knows a lot. He mentioned colours I'd never even heard of."

Neil laughed. "Do you think there are colours we've never encountered?"

"We may have encountered them, but we may not have a name for them. Then we get a name, and suddenly we see that those colours have been around us all along. There they are."

He asked her what she was going to do with the knowledge she picked up on the course. "You're not going to give up microbiology, surely? Not entirely."

"I may."

"It would seem such a waste. All that studying. All those examinations. The PhD—the lot."

She said that science would probably get by without her. "And plenty of people get a PhD and then file it away in a drawer. Edinburgh's full of drawers stuffed with PhDs."

He smiled. "We'll see."

She finished preparing the moussaka. Later, as they ate it, he said, "I'd love to go to Greece, wouldn't you? To the same place we went before. That house."

"With the olive trees and that donkey that kept braying?"

"Yes, and with the priest in the village with his dirty beard."

Chrissie smiled at the memory. "He had crumbs in it, remember? It looked like crumbs of feta cheese had lodged in his beard."

"Feta?"

"Yes. And I'm sure I saw a bit of an olive too."

Neil said that he did not know why religions laid such store by beards. Was it a sign of holiness—whatever that was? She laughed. "It must be for the same reason they insist that people shouldn't eat certain things."

"That's to bring people together," Neil suggested. "If you all don't eat sausages, or whatever, then you have that bond between you. You can say: we are the people who don't eat sausages—or cornflakes, or whatever it is."

She looked at him intently. "You know something, Neil? I've never asked you this, but do you believe in God? Isn't it odd? We've never talked about that." She paused. "It really is odd, when you come to think of it. People don't ask their friends that question."

"Perhaps they assume. If you live in a society like ours—today— you just assume that everyone is a rational materialist."

She frowned. "But you haven't answered my question."

He held her gaze. There was a bit of him that wanted to say yes, but he felt constrained by embarrassment. It was a strangely intimate question, it seemed to him. "Not really," he said at last. "I can't believe in somebody up there looking down on us." That was true, he thought: the white-bearded God made no sense.

"No. I can't either."

He looked down at his hands. There was purpose in the world. Human hands had a purpose. They had a design. And he remembered seeing a hospital chaplain holding the hand of a patient who had only hours to live.

"I suppose I'm like most people we know," he began. "And yet, sometimes I feel something in me that I can't explain. I feel something *might* be there. Some guiding force. Something that makes the whole thing work."

She nodded. "I know what you mean. And I suppose you could call that spirit—or God, if you like. What do the Hindus call it? Brahman? Universal spirit. The force behind everything."

"Perhaps we have to believe in something like that," he went on. "If we don't, then there's no reason for anything. We can do as we wish. We can do anything, because nothing has ultimate meaning." He looked at her. "And there are practical considerations. How could we trust anybody if nothing has any meaning beyond the . . . beyond the immediate, I suppose?"

She became still. She had her fork in her hand. It was just above the tablecloth. He saw a vein on the side of her neck move almost imperceptibly with her pulse. "Trust?" she asked.

"Yes, trust. We have to have a basis for trust, because if we don't . . . well, nothing would work. Trust has to be the foundation of everything."

She shrugged. "Possibly." She lowered her fork onto the plate. "Greece," she said.

He smiled. "I'm in favour of Greece."

He lay beside her in bed. Through a chink in the curtains, light from the street outside made a pattern on the ceiling. He looked at her: her breathing was regular, and he knew that she was asleep. He did not feel at all tired. His mind was active. He knew that it could be hours before he fell asleep.

She stirred in her sleep; her arm moved slightly under the sheet, and then was still. She looked so vulnerable—as all sleepers do. Even tyrants must sleep, he thought; and they were, in their sleeping hours, no stronger than any of their subjects. Sleep equalised us all. He looked at her, and thought of how precious she was to him. She was.

She had said to him, as he switched out the light, "I'm really tired. Do you mind? You don't mind, do you?"

He had said, "Of course not," and had kissed her gently before turning away. Why, he thought, do we need other people, when life without emotional entanglements must be so much simpler? It seemed that he needed Chrissie, but he wondered whether this was just out of habit. The people we had in our lives were sometimes there because they were habits into which we had gradually grown. That was, he thought, a rather bleak conclusion—and he made an effort to put it out of his mind.

He closed his eyes, as sleep slowly pulled its blanket over him. But then he opened them again in the darkness, staring up at the ceiling, on which a gap in the curtains had traced a faint pattern of light. He remembered their conversation from earlier that evening, when she had urged him to stand his ground and defy Henrietta. Why had she done that? It was not that long ago that she had expressed sympathy for Henrietta, who, she said, had had to struggle to get where she got to, whose ruthlessness had to be admired. Now she was advising him to confront her, and had been dismissive of the risk that such defiance entailed. Why?

He had no answer. He felt himself drifting off to sleep. By his side, Chrissie stirred, and ground her teeth almost soundlessly. Bruxism. He would speak to her about it, along with so much else that they needed to discuss.

Seven

Neil cycled to work whenever possible, only using the car on those days on which he found himself behind schedule, or when the weather was particularly wet. Rain came in from the west—sweeping in from the Atlantic and crossing the country in white veils or, cold and insistent, from the North Sea, drenching Scotland in unseasonable icy downpours. On such days, Neil would drive in with Chrissie, he at the wheel while she finished her coffee and toast in the passenger seat. He said to her, "You should get up earlier," and she smiled, and told him that he should drive in such a way as not to spill her coffee.

On that morning, though, the sky was clear, and Neil set off on his bicycle, following a back road that led to the institute's buildings next to the medical school. He was early, and the traffic was light. The side roads seemed deserted, and he reached his destination within fifteen minutes of leaving the flat. He dismounted and secured his bike in one of the racks near the side door. Then he turned round, bent down to remove his cycle clips, and found himself facing Tom Barnes.

Tom had also arrived by bike, and was now making his way towards the front entrance. He was reading a message on his phone, and so he almost collided with Neil, whom he had not seen. Both stood quite still.

Neil hesitated. He had no desire to speak to Tom, and knew, too, that it would be unwise to approach him while he was suspended. At the back of his mind was a vague memory about not speaking to witnesses in criminal proceedings—something half picked up from crime dramas on television—but now that they were facing one another directly it was hardly possible for him to ignore the young man's existence.

They stared at one another, each equally surprised. Neil, though, sensed that he had the advantage: he was more experienced—this young man was a student, and he—Neil—was the victim of, at the very least, a mistake on his part. If anybody had grounds to feel awkward, it was Tom, not him.

"Good morning. It's Tom, isn't it?"

Tom hesitated, as if he might not be quite certain of his name. Eventually he replied, "Yes, it is."

Neil felt his heart beating hard within him. He had not antici-pated this confrontation, but now it seemed to him to be inevitable. And why should he not confront the source of the trouble in which he had become embroiled? "You made a complaint, I believe."

The effect was immediate. Tom looked away sharply. He said nothing.

"You're not denying it," Neil pressed.

The silence persisted.

"I think that you misunderstood what I said in that lecture," Neil said at last, his confidence growing. "I referred to disgusting condi-tions, not to disgusting people."

Tom turned his head slightly. He gave Neil a resentful look. "You can't get out of it that easily."

Neil drew in his breath. "Has it occurred to you that you might have misheard me? Has it occurred to you that you might be in the wrong here?"

Tom blinked. "Why should I be wrong? I heard what you said. Now you come along and deny it—well, I heard it." He paused. "How do you think I felt?"

Neil shook his head. "How did you feel? I don't see what your feelings have got to do with it. Even if I said what you accuse me of saying, how would that have anything to do with your feelings?"

The answer came quickly. "I felt unsafe. I'm entitled to feel safe in lectures." Now came the challenge: "How can anybody feel safe in a lecture room where the lecturer is capable of holding opinions like that?"

Neil felt a surge of anger within him. "I do not hold those opinions, Tom. Can't you see that? You misunderstood me. I don't think of people living in squalid conditions as being disgusting. I just don't. I regard it as disgusting that they are obliged to live like that." He gave Tom a searching look. "Can't you grasp the distinction?"

Tom looked away again. Then he took a step forward to get past. As he did so, he pushed against Neil, as if to move him out of the way. Neil gave a push back. Their conversation was not finished, and he wanted his accuser to understand just how wrong he had been.

"You're assaulting me," Tom hissed.

"I'm not," said Neil. "You pushed me."

"I didn't."

"This is ridiculous," Neil countered, stepping to the side.

Tom walked off. Neil wanted to shout out after him, but he did not. He went to let himself into his office. Struggling to control his breathing, he sat down at his desk. Was this what it was like to experience the precursor of a heart attack—this sudden shortage of air? He looked up at the ceiling, and realised that he had never before looked at the ceiling of his office. He had seen it, he supposed, but he had never looked at it as he looked at it now. He saw that there was a crack zigzagging from a corner to the light fitting in the centre. The building had been constructed in the nineteen-seventies, when new buildings were often shoddy, erected with scant regard to the future. This was such a building, and there were other signs of gimcrack economies: the cladding on one section had been replaced, and then the replacement had itself cracked and allowed moisture to enter. Eventually the whole place would have to be knocked down, an architect friend had told him.

After ten minutes or so he calmed down. He reached for a file that he had left on his desk, and opened it. It contained a copy of a report on the impact of Lyme disease. He glanced at the names of the authors, and realised he knew two of them from conferences he had attended. He began to read the summary: *From being a disease occurring within a restricted geographical area, the range of Lyme disease has extended in recent years to the point where governments are beginning to take notice of the potential of this tick-borne infection to cause—*

A knock on his door made him look up. And then the door opened, before he had time to react. Henrietta stood before him, staring at him wordlessly. Neil returned her gaze. It was obvious to him what had happened; he had half expected it.

"I've had Tom Barnes in my office a few moments ago," she said.

Neil shrugged. "Yes, I saw him outside."

"He tells me that you assaulted him."

Neil closed his eyes. Of course Tom Barnes would tell Henrietta that he had been assaulted. He should not be surprised by this.

He tried not to sound weary. "I didn't. Believe me: I did not assault Tom Barnes. I just didn't."

Henrietta's eyes narrowed. "You say you didn't assault him?"

"That's what I said. He gave me a push—something like that. I pushed past him—after he pushed against me."

Henrietta was shaking her head. "This is very, very serious."

Neil closed the file on his desk, obscuring the paper on Lyme disease. Lyme disease mattered—it counted for something; this playground spat was completely unimportant. He wanted to say that to Henrietta. He wanted to say: "For heaven's sake, try to get a sense of proportion."

But she precluded any response from him. "This really needs to be dealt with at a higher level," she said. "I can't deal with this myself; the board must be involved." She paused. There was real anger in her expression now. Prior to this, he thought, she probably did not really believe in what she was saying. Hers was the language of shibboleths and bureaucratic formulae; it was not a language in which its users actually believed.

"So what do you want me to do?" asked Neil. "This student's got it in for me. Can't you see that?"

She shook her head. "I don't think you understand what's happening here."

"But I do," Neil replied. "I understand it rather better than you imagine. And I understand, too, that you're not on my side—definitely not. I'm a member of your staff, and I'm being given no support in circumstances where my ability to do my job is being threatened."

Henrietta did not respond immediately, but then she said, "He said that I revealed his identity to you. He's accusing me of a breach of confidence."

Neil could not help but laugh. "You're the one being accused of something now? Well, that's outrageous."

She ignored the taunt. "I suggest that you leave the office," she said. "I think you shouldn't come into the building until this matter is resolved. In fact, that's an instruction, not a suggestion."

He stood up. "I'd never ignore an instruction of yours, Henrietta. Message received."

He picked up the bag beside his desk and began to make his way towards the door. Henrietta stepped aside to let him get past. Neither spoke.

Outside, he was struck by the brightness of the daylight. It was early May, and spring was struggling to impose its authority. Yet now, for the first time that year, Neil felt that the dreary cloak of the winter months had been convincingly put back in the cupboard. He stood for a moment outside the front door of the institute and let the sun touch his face with its warmth. There was a life outside the petty oppressiveness of academic politics—the arguments, the self-importance, the hectoring. He looked about him at the purposeful world: the world of people going to work on the bus that lumbered past, the world of the man cutting the hedge on the other side of the street, the world of the delivery truck waiting at the lights, having somewhere to go. Did the people doing these things worry about feeling safe?

He went to retrieve his bicycle and began his ride back to the flat, not pedalling at all fast, sitting back and letting the air rush past him, not needing, nor wanting, to get home particularly fast. He was in no hurry, because his life was *in suspension*. He smiled at the thought: this was the suspended life—which was actually rather unstressful and not all that unpleasant. He thought of the flat. Chrissie had said that she would be at a meeting all day; he would be alone until she came back, but he might go to the shops and get something for their dinner. He might also clean the bathroom, which would be a nice surprise for her, because she had commented on the fact that it was looking dirty: *manky* was the word she used. It was his toothpaste, she said, half accusingly, that made such a mess, because it was pink and left its mark in a way in which well-behaved white toothpastes did not. He had defended it: pink toothpaste had a refreshing taste to it, and an unthreatening, old-fashioned name, Euthymol. She had laughed, and accused him of being sentimental about toothpaste. "There are far better causes to be sentimental about," she said.

He went into the flat, tossing his bag down on the chair near the door. He stretched. Home. That ghastly Henrietta. She was Medusa. A Gorgon. And that deluded boy. And the Greek chorus that seemed intent on hounding him for something he had not said. It was a Kafkaesque nightmare, but it was real, and it was happening to him.

He decided to change into his gym kit. He would go to the gym and work through his anger. The gym was good for that.

He went towards the bedroom. The door was closed. He pushed it. Something resisted on the other side. He was puzzled. He pushed again, and the door yielded.

Chrissie was wearing a dressing gown. When he saw her, the first thought that came into his mind was: why was she here, at this hour of the morning? She had said she would be at a meeting, and had told him what it would be—the environmental committee she served on, or was it . . . Then he saw the man standing behind her. He had slicked-down hair, though a strand had strayed across his forehead. Unexpectedly at such a moment, he noticed details. The front of this man's shirt was undone; he saw that the collar was one of those button-down types. He was not wearing shoes.

Chrissie gasped. She had been trying to stop the door being opened, pushing her weight against it in a desperate attempt to prevent this exposure.

Neil looked at her. He knew who this was. This was the interior design tutor, and for a few moments he struggled to recall the name. It came to him: Brian. This was Brian, who she had said had such a good eye. The shirt was just the sort of shirt that an interior design tutor would wear. Of course it was him.

The man grimaced. He met Neil's gaze briefly, before he looked down to his stockinged feet, as if they were the cause of this embarrassment. Chrissie's lip quivered. She gathered the dressing gown about her, shreds of modesty under the spotlight of this moment of revelation.

Neil opened his mouth to say something, but closed it again, wordlessly.

She said, "Oh, Neil—"

He stopped her with a motion of his hand. She gave a start, as if she feared he would strike her. He would never do that, of course, but he found himself thinking: what would other men do? Was this the sort of situation where, with other players, violence would occur?

He took a step back, almost tripping over himself.

She said, once again, "Neil . . ."

This, he thought, is what a vacuum feels like: empty, composed of nothing.

Brian left, still struggling to put on his jacket. Neil noticed its colour: a mustard of a shade that he had always found distasteful. *She had a lover who wore a mustard-coloured jacket* . . . A little, irrelevant detail, he thought, that added to the picture.

Neil stared at Chrissie. He noticed that she had picked up a tube of peppermints and had extracted one to put into her mouth. He could not imagine why she should do that at such a time. She had just been caught cheating, and she chose to eat a peppermint . . .

He closed his eyes. The betrayal hit him with an almost physical force. "How could you?" he stuttered.

He looked at her. Her reaction was to suck harder on the peppermint, pulling in her cheeks, fixing him with a cold, unemotional stare. She seemed to be weighing up what he had said, as if assessing the words for accuracy or justification.

"That's what men say," she retorted. "You're saying exactly what men say when women express themselves sexually. You don't like it."

He gasped. He was not sure where to begin, and what he said next appeared unconnected with what had gone before.

"What do you believe in?" he asked.

She looked puzzled. "What do you mean by that?"

"I mean: what do you believe in?"

She shrugged. She was not going to attempt to answer his question. "I can understand why you're upset. You don't need to be, you know. Open relationships are a sign of maturity."

He felt his heart hammering within him. He felt a sudden urge to grab her physically, to bring her cool detachment to an end. He felt ashamed. It was alien to his nature to engage in confrontation. The whole business with Henrietta had gone against the grain, and the same was true of this. This simply was not him.

"I'm leaving," he muttered.

"I'm sorry you're taking it this way," she said.

E i g h t

James showed him the room.

"I hardly ever use it," he said. "Occasionally, when people turn up in Edinburgh, they stay here for a day or two, but that doesn't happen very often." He paused. "Do you remember Malcolm Ferguson? From our year? He became an orthopaedic surgeon somewhere in the north of England . . ."

"Durham."

"Yes, somewhere like that."

"It was Durham," said Neil. "I saw him there when I went on a course. He had acquired a wife and two sets of twins. Two."

James smiled. "Sounds like carelessness."

"He was keen on horse racing. He used to read a racing paper in lectures."

James nodded. "He stayed with me for a couple of days once, some time ago—when he was still working in Glasgow. Before the two sets of twins. Four kids! And Julia Christopherson. You might know her perhaps. She's a toxicologist."

"I've met her," said Neil. "I don't really know her."

"Well, she stayed here for a month, maybe a bit more. She put those curtains up because I didn't have any in here at the time. There was a Venetian blind which didn't work very well. Julia went out and bought those curtains from an Oxfam shop. She was proud of finding some that were an exact fit."

Neil looked about the room. There was a bed with a cover of checked material. There was a table near the window, and a bookcase, with a radio on top of it. On the wall facing the bed was a larger framed print of a sailing ship under attack by a French man-of-war. Long, trailing flags flew on both vessels; the symbols for which men died at sea.

He turned to James. "You're very kind."

James shook his head. "It's no trouble." He looked at Neil. "I'm sorry about your . . . your situation."

Neil thanked him. "Just for a night or two. I don't want to put you out."

"You won't be putting me out. I told you: this is what the room is for."

"For waifs and strays?"

"I wouldn't call you that," said James. "For the temporarily homeless, perhaps."

Neil glanced at his watch, automatically, as he had no need to check the time. It was six o'clock, not much more than eight hours since he had walked out of his flat—Chrissie's flat, he reminded himself—carrying a hastily packed bag. The bag contained shorts, pants, socks. He had bundled in a jacket, too, and a toiletry bag stuffed with a razor, shaving cream, his pink Euthymol toothpaste. He would have to go back some time to retrieve other possessions, but this was all that he needed now in the aftermath of the morning's events.

He had called James, who was the first person he thought of. He could have contacted other friends, but James seemed the right person to get in touch with because his other friends had spouses or partners and would probably find it more difficult to take in somebody arriving on their doorstep with no notice. As Neil had expected, James did not even have to be asked. "Come to my place," he had said. "You can stay. I've got a clinic this afternoon, which I shouldn't cancel, but I'll be back early evening. Will you survive until then?"

He had assured him he would, and they had rung off. He had a few hours to kill, and so he had gone to a cinema and bought himself a ticket. They had looked suspiciously at his bag, but had allowed him to store it during the film. He took in nothing of what was happening on the screen, his mind in turmoil. The discovery of Chrissie's unfaithfulness was a bolt out of the blue. I had no idea, he said to himself. But then he remembered the conversation they had once had about reliability, and how she had changed the subject. He had experienced a moment of doubt then, and perhaps for good reason.

It was strange, though, that he should be surprised. Surely people in his position, people who discovered that their partners were having an affair, would have an inkling of what was going on. You would expect there to be some sign of dissatisfaction or unhappiness. Surely there would be arguments, rows, moodiness—anything to give a warning that all was not well. There had been none of that.

Of course, people stumbled across clues. There might be an overlooked note, or lipstick on a handkerchief, or an email that somebody thought had been deleted but that was still there. Women found hairs of a different colour on their husbands' jackets. That was a classic device in stories of adultery. A blonde hair—part of the unfair stereotype of the blonde seductress, the blonde other woman. Far more likely was the indiscreet email. Blonde hairs on shoulders happened mostly in fiction; indiscreet emails happened in real life, and had been behind the break-up, Neil now reminded himself, of a friend's relationship. She had told him that she had discovered what her boyfriend was doing when she had switched on his laptop computer without his permission. He was out of the flat and she needed to look something up online. The computer was sitting on the kitchen table; her own laptop had developed a fault and was awaiting repair. She remembered his password because she had told him it was insufficiently secure. "You should never use the name of your street," she had said. "It's far too obvious." Now she typed it in, and the offending email came up on the screen, having just arrived.

"You're well rid of him," Neil had said. He had never liked her boyfriend, who drove a red Porsche with an unnecessary throaty roar. An email like that was only to be expected.

He imagined that Chrissie had exchanged emails with Brian—some of them to do with the course he was running. But there would have been others. He found himself wondering when they had been able to see one another. Had it always been during the day, when he thought that she was at work? That might have been difficult, because they worked, after all, in the same building and he often saw her during the day. It would have been far easier if their workplaces had been completely different.

He tried to remember whether she had been out much in the evenings. Now that he applied his mind to it, he could see a pattern emerging. There were her Pilates sessions; she had joined a book group; she had gone out on several girls' evenings, with old school friends, she had said. These friends made up the centre of her social circle: they had dinner together; they went to each other's houses. Sometimes this had been on the evenings when he was playing squash with James. Then he had been off at a conference, which had meant he had been away for three days over a weekend. He had phoned her on the Saturday evening and she had not replied, which had puzzled him briefly, but he had soon forgotten about it. She had said that her phone had been turned off; but why had she done that? She usually left her phone on while she was in the flat. That must have been because she was meeting Brian. It was obvious now.

James handed him a key. "Here we are," he said. "This is for the front door."

Neil thanked him. He was embarrassed by the readiness and generosity of James's welcome. He said, "You're a good friend, James."

James made little of it. "You'd do the same for me."

Neil hoped that he would, but he could not be sure. It was the ultimate test of friendship, really—the moment when the need of a friend was for a bed and a roof. That was the point at which a shallow friendship might reach breaking point.

"Do you want to talk?" James asked. "You don't have to, you know."

Neil hesitated, and then nodded. "Chrissie has been having an affair. I couldn't stay in the flat."

James agreed. "That would be difficult." He waited.

"She's been doing a class on interior design. She has a tutor called Brian . . ."

"Brian," muttered James.

"Yes, and he's become her lover, it seems."

James absorbed this. "How did you find out?" No sooner had he asked the question than he regretted it. Now he said, "Sorry, I don't mean to pry. You don't need to say anything."

Neil assured him that he did not mind. "In fact," he said, "it probably helps to let somebody else know."

James listened as Neil recounted the events of that morning. "It was in the flat," he said. "That's what hurts most, I suppose—the fact that they were in our bedroom."

James shook his head. "Not very . . ." He seemed to struggle for the right words. "Not very considerate."

"That's putting it mildly," said Neil.

James looked thoughtful. "I can't imagine what it must be like to two-time somebody," he said. "I can see how people move on, so to speak, from one person to another. That's easy enough to understand: you meet somebody and you fall in love with them, and you're still with somebody else. So you end it. But carrying on with another person while you're still sleeping with the first person . . . I don't get that, I'm afraid."

Neil said that he thought that this is exactly what a lot of people do. "When you hear about married people having affairs, that's more or less what's happening. They keep two relationships going at the same time."

"Well, I don't think I could," James said.

Neil looked at his friend. He did not think James could, either. And yet he knew relatively little about this man with whom he played squash each week. Did he know anything about James's emotional life—other than that he was gay and that he did not have a partner at the moment, as far as he knew?

"You're a faithful type, then," Neil said. "There must be two sorts of people, it seems: those who are faithful, and those who aren't." He thought about this as he spoke, and realised that this was probably far too simple. Human behaviour was too complicated to allow for a simple dividing in this way.

James was smiling. "Faithful? Yes. No choice. There are those who don't have much choice. They're faithful because there's no alternative. They might be keen to be unfaithful, if you see what I mean, but the opportunity might never present itself. So they remain faithful."

"Possibly," said Neil. He stared at his friend, unsure as to whether he could take this conversation further. He had never discussed sex with James—other than in the most general, abstract terms; he had never enquired as to his relationships, if he had any, which was always possible. There were people who kept to themselves; some who never entered into any sexual relationships with others because they simply did not want to. Some people were fastidious; others were simply not interested because they felt no drive to be involved; some people were afraid.

Neil decided to ask. "Have you got somebody? Do you mind if I ask—maybe you do. In which case, ignore the question. It's none of my business, I suppose."

There was no sign that James had taken offence. He held Neil's gaze as he answered. "No. Not really."

"Not really?"

"I said not really because there isn't anybody with whom I can say I'm in a relationship—or at least not a relationship of the sort you're talking about. But that doesn't mean that there isn't anybody. There is—sort of."

Neil was ready to bring this conversation to an end; he did not want to intrude, and it made him feel slightly awkward pressing James on what could be for him an entirely private matter. Not everybody liked to lay bare their heart. But James, it seemed, was happy to continue.

"There is somebody I like," he said. He smiled. "That sounds really coy, doesn't it? *Somebody I like.* I should say to you, *somebody I love*, but I find that a bit hard, to tell the truth. *Love* is a big word for me. And a hard one, too."

"Because you're used to other people expecting you not to love the people you love? Is that it? Because people aren't prepared to accept that you can feel the way you do about love?" He paused. "I can understand that. I can imagine that's not easy."

"No, it isn't," said James. "It's as if we're speaking totally different languages. Gay people speak one language, and straight people speak another. It's a bit like that."

"Does it have to be?"

James sighed. "Of course not. There are a lot of things that don't have to be the way they are, but nonetheless that's the way they are. I can't make them any different just because I think they're wrong the way they are at the moment. We live with the way other people think about things. Everybody does that—ultimately."

"So?" said Neil.

"So?"

"Yes," Neil continued. "You said that there was somebody you liked. Is that it? Can't you do anything about it?"

"In a word, no," said James. "I'd like to, but I can't." He paused, and then retracted part of what he had said. "I said I'd like to do something, but that might not mean I'd like to do what you think I might like to do." He smiled. "This is getting a bit complicated, isn't it?"

"It is," agreed Neil. "But then that's exactly what human life is—complicated."

"What I'm trying to say," James went on, "is that it's impossible. It can't be what I might want it to be. I mean, this other person. He can't be anything other than what *he* is, and I can't be anything other than what *I* am."

Neil waited.

"He's not interested, you see."

Neil understood. "I see. Sorry, I was a bit slow on the uptake. I should have realised that that was what you were trying to say."

James said that there was no need to apologise. He was used to people not realising. "Although that sounds a bit arrogant on my part—and I don't mean to be. But it is true, you know: many people don't get that particular bit. They're used to things being at least possible, even if they don't work out. They aren't used to things that *can't be*. That's the issue."

"I see."

"So there I am," James continued. "I'm in love with somebody who can't love me back. What do you call that? Unrequited love? Yes, sure, it's that all right. But it's a bit more than that. It's *impossible*. It just can't be."

Neil waited for a few moments before he spoke. The revelation made by James was a profound one: it deserved space. "And you never told him?" he asked at last.

James shook his head. "Do you think I should have?"

"Well, how else would you know that it could never be?"

"You know these things. You always do. A lot of what we know, we know by instinct."

Neil stared down at the rug at his feet. It was an old tribal piece, as Chrissie would put it. She had probably picked that term up from Brian, who was a consultant to a rug gallery. She had said something about that, but he had not been listening and he could not recall what it was. *He had not been listening* . . . Relationships floundered on precisely that failing, he thought. People did not listen to one another, and then were surprised by the turn of events.

He glanced at James. He, too, was looking elsewhere as he spoke: that was the point about the Catholic confessional, Neil thought suddenly—you could unburden yourself without looking at the priest. It was easier that way. The Catholic Church understood how people felt about these things; it knew well what unburdening meant.

"I'll tell you about it one day," James said. "Or I may not. It depends." He gave Neil a quizzical look. "I never assume that people want to hear about what's going on in my life, particularly if things aren't going well."

Neil agreed. "Nobody really enjoys the misery memoir."

They had been standing at the entrance to the spare room. Now James crossed the floor and switched on a table lamp. "I had this lamp when I was a student," he said. "I was so proud of it. It's Danish. I went without lunch for a whole week in order to be able to pay for it."

"Going without lunch is character-building," said Neil.

James turned to him. "Everything's happening to you at once, isn't it? I mean, you have Henrietta after you, and now this." He shook his head. "Chrissie's timing's brilliant. You're facing a full-frontal attack at work and she opens up another front. A great strategy."

Neil looked thoughtful. "Yes, it's not ideal."

James was incredulous. "Not ideal? That's a bit of an understatement. How did Harold Macmillan describe political disaster: *little local difficulties?*"

"It was probably going on before all this started."

"She's on good terms with Henrietta, though," observed James. "That surprised me."

It took Neil a little while to react. He had not anticipated this: Chrissie saw Henrietta in the same light as he did, or so he assumed. They had talked about her and there was nothing to suggest otherwise. "No," he said at last. "I don't think she is."

"But . . ." James began, and then stopped himself.

Neil looked at him expectantly. James looked away. "Maybe I'm wrong." He glanced at Neil as if weighing up whether to continue. "It's just that I saw them the other day. It was lunchtime. They were having lunch together in that vegetarian takeaway place. They have a couple of tables at the back. They were there. I was collecting a sandwich. They were having coffee together. They were deep in conversation."

Neil was silent.

James continued hesitantly. "They looked like two friends having lunch together—not two enemies." He paused. "I don't suppose enemies have lunch together, do they? Perhaps they were discussing work. Are they involved in a project together?"

Neil shook his head. "No, they aren't. Henrietta does very little research these days. She does a bit of teaching and the rest of her time is spent on administration."

James nodded. "George Bernard Shaw," he said.

"Why him?"

James smiled. "He said: those who can, do; those who can't,

teach. It's the same with research, I think. Those who can research, do it; those who can't, administer. That's Henrietta's profile. There are plenty of people like her."

Neil wondered why Chrissie had said nothing about the lunch. They did not tell one another everything, but he always mentioned it when he met one of his friends socially—and she had done the same, he thought. It occurred to him that she might have taken it upon herself to mediate in some way—perhaps even to plead with Henrietta to drop the whole apology idea. That was possible, but it seemed, on balance, to be rather unlikely.

James had asked him a question that he had missed. "I'm sorry," he said. "I was thinking."

"I wondered what you were going to do?"

Neil still sounded detached. "To do about what?"

"What are you going to do about that complaint? I take it you're going to fight it. I would if I were you."

Later, Neil would ask himself why he answered so quickly. It was the defining moment, and he spoke firmly, as one who has gone over all the possibilities and alighted on one that has to be chosen. Chrissie's affair was the final straw. He did not have the energy to do anything now; he was defeated.

"I'm resigning," he said. "Tomorrow."

They stared at one another. For a while, nothing was said. James thought they were standing in the wreckage of a career; that was how it felt to him.

Then Neil went on, "I'm going to take a break. I'm going to go away somewhere."

James absorbed this. Then he asked, "Are you sure?"

"Absolutely. I've made up my mind."

"Where will you go?"

"I'll find somewhere," said Neil. He had not given it any thought. "I'll rent somewhere in the Highlands. I'll get away from things."

James looked concerned. "You can stay here if you like."

"That's kind of you," said Neil. "But I want a change." He shrugged. "I just feel the need to get away from all . . . from all this."

"All this what?" asked James.

"All this . . . conflict—if that's the word." He paused. "I feel as if I've stumbled out of a world in which people liked one another . . ." He shrugged. "Into a world where everybody is at one another's throats, if you see what I mean. Suddenly it seems to be war—and I want to get away from it."

James was looking at him. "Loads of bad karma," he said.

Neil nodded. "You could put it that way. There's a lot of poison."

A thought suddenly occurred to him: was he unattractive to Chrissie? Had she gone off him? Was it that simple—or that sordid? It could be a purely physical matter; perhaps Brian could offer something that he could not—it could be that, which was not an easy conclusion for one who had been rejected. It was humiliating, because none of us wanted to feel unattractive in that sense. That was the last conclusion we wanted to draw.

Neil sensed that James understood. That was a concomitant of the way he looked at the world, he thought; James had a heightened degree of sensitivity to the emotions of others. Or were any claims to that effect gay exceptionalism, Neil wondered. Not everyone would agree that being gay gave you an insight that many others might lack, but it was probably true. People like James *bothered* to empathise. How could you not empathise when you were, in your very essence, subtly excluded, even in liberal societies that had put persecution behind them? And even if being gay in itself did not give people a special perspective, then how others reacted to your sexual identity would have that effect.

James crossed the room to look out of the window. The rooftops glistened in the rain. The midday sun played on the wet cobblestones on the street below.

"The Highlands?"

"Yes. Anywhere. Maybe even one of the islands. Skye. Tiree. I don't mind."

James turned around to face him. "You know, I have a place up there. On the island of Mull. It belonged to my grandfather. He was born up there, as was my father. They bought it twenty years ago and then gave it to me about five years ago. A small farmhouse— nothing special. So we have a family link up there. One foot on Mull, so to speak."

Neil did not know that.

"I hardly ever use it," said James. "I haven't been up there for months. Sometimes my cousins stay in it for a few weeks over the summer, but they've gone to live in Boston for a couple of years. My parents both died, as I think you know."

Neil remembered. It had been hard for James: his parents both became ill within a few months of one another, in one of those odd demographic events when an entire generation of a family dies at much the same time.

"The house is pretty basic," James continued. "But it's there if you're interested. It would do it good to be lived in, for a change. Houses get damp if they're left empty."

It was Neil's second spur-of-the-moment decision of the day. "Are you sure?" he asked.

James shrugged. "Yes. If you want it, it's yours for as long as you need it."

"I do," said Neil. "I mean, I would. I'd like it—as long as that's okay with you."

"Perfect," said James.

"I'll pay rent," said Neil.

"No, you won't. I won't accept it."

Neil smiled. "I feel that I should have given the matter more thought."

"Unnecessary," said James. "Some things are best acted upon on impulse." He glanced briefly at Neil, and added, "A lot of things, actually."

James left the room to return with a photograph. He handed this to Neil. "This is it. Taken last summer when I was there for a week."

Neil looked at the picture. A small house, whitewashed in the way of the west coast of Scotland, stood a few hundred yards from the shore of a sea-loch. Behind it a hill rose sharply to a cloudless sky. There was a shed and what looked like a barn or boathouse behind the house. There were trees further along the shore, a mixture of broadleaf and Scots pine. No other houses were in sight.

"Isolated enough?" asked James. "You said you wanted to get away."

Neil nodded.

"The water supply comes from the burn." James pointed to the line of the water course, marked with shrubs and occasional trees. At a point further up the hill it became a small waterfall, a wisp of white.

"There's electricity," said James. "You're just close enough to the village to get that. It's five miles down that track. There, behind the house."

James gave Neil a searching look. "You might see nobody for days on end," he said, adding, "Perhaps that's what you want, of course. You could lick your wounds up there. It's a good place for that."

Neil managed a weak smile. "It's not that bad. I'm all right." He disliked self-pity in others and would not allow it in himself.

"You can change your mind," James assured him.

"I don't think I will," said Neil, taking his phone out of his pocket. "I'm going to send a resignation email right now."

James looked alarmed. "This may be a case for the *don't send* button," he said. "Or the *recall* one."

Neil shook his head. "It's a long time since I've felt so certain about anything," he said.

James started to say something, but stopped. He had never believed it possible to convince others about very much—people, it seemed to him, made up their own minds and were, in general, unlikely to listen to the advice of others, including that of their friends. "You don't have to stay up there," he said. "If a couple of days are enough, no disaster. You're welcome back here any time. I hope you know that."

Neil thanked him. He would give it a try, he said.

They went into the kitchen, where James made coffee. As he poured, he said, "So she's getting away with it." His tone was regretful, not angry.

Neil stared into his mug. "I'm sorry, I just don't feel in the mood for a fight. Some other time, maybe. Not now."

James nodded. "I understand. But people are never stopped, are they?" He paused. "I'm not criticising you."

"I didn't think you were. But you're right, anyway. Perhaps more people should have stood up to the Spanish Inquisition."

"But they did," said James. "And that's why they burned them at the stake. The worst death imaginable."

Neil made a gesture of helplessness. "So long ago," he said.

"Yesterday," said James.

While James made dinner, Neil unpacked his bag in his room. He would need to get more clothes, he thought, as he had not brought many. Yet he was not sure he could face Chrissie just yet. And what if Brian had moved in? He did not imagine he could go back in such circumstances, even to gather up his possessions. Perhaps James would go round to collect them for him.

He thought of Chrissie, even though he did not want to. Thinking of her made him feel sick in his stomach—a curious sensation that was not disgust, but was not far from it. Contrasting feelings could be so close on the emotional spectrum: fear and elation; joy and sorrow—a narrow borderland lay between them. This feeling was rawness, as if something had been ripped from him: rawness and emptiness. How could she hurt him like this? It must be because he did not mean very much to her—that was the only explanation. And how could she have lunch with Henrietta when she knew what Henrietta was doing to him at work? Unless, of course, she and Henrietta were friends and allies all along—which meant that Chrissie might even be party to what Henrietta was doing. The thought appalled him. It was impossible. Yet it made sense. If Chrissie wanted him out of her life, then it made perfect sense for her to do something to get him out of their mutual workplace. That, though, presumed a ruthlessness on her part which he could not imagine she possessed. Yet she had been with Brian in *their* flat, in *their* bed, he imagined. How could she? Easily, he thought. Sex trumped everything, it seemed. It was quite capable of destroying anything: marriage, friendships, ambitions, careers, empires.

He sat down at the desk and stared out of the window. His view was of a tenement rooftop, of chimney stacks and grey slate, and of a gull, wheeling and mewing in the wind. He struggled to control his feelings. It would be only too easy to become paranoid, and to imagine Henrietta and Chrissie plotting together—and with that boy too, Tom Barnes, who could be part and parcel of their scheme, whatever it was, persuaded for some obscure and tortuous reason to bring a groundless complaint.

He allowed himself to explore that dangerous avenue. It was feasible, even if somewhat far-fetched, but if it was true, then he had played into their hands in exactly the way they intended.

He got up from his chair. He would go into the kitchen and help James. Guests should offer to help: it was a basic social rule. They should offer to help and they should not stay for more than three days. That suited him. He would make the journey to Mull the day after tomorrow. He would buy provisions, get a new set of walking boots and a thick sweater, and make the journey to that white-painted farmhouse, in which Henrietta would become a distant memory, and even Chrissie might be forgotten, at least in part, if not entirely. He could not imagine himself obliterating her from his memory: surely you could not forget a lover unless you had an utterly cold heart. Perhaps that was what she had, and Henrietta, too. That made him think again of their collusion, and the more he thought of it, the more likely it seemed to him, and the more shocking. Disloyalty was too weak a word for that sort of thing—treachery fitted rather better. Abandonment. Desertion. There was a whole glossary of terms to describe what Chrissie had done, but . . . Here he stopped, and wondered whether she saw herself in those terms. She probably did not. She would say that there was her side to the story, and that her involvement with Brian was not something for which she needed to apologise. People met other people who simply meant more to them than the person they were with. It was as simple as that. People fell out of love with the same arbitrariness and unexpectedness, and it was unrealistic, if not actually cruel, to ask them to stay with somebody whom they no longer loved. Perhaps she would say that she had fallen out of love with him because of the way he behaved. People who left other people often rewrote the history of the relationship so that they might seem justified. She might be tempted to do just that, and to portray him as controlling, or dependent, or insensitive to her needs: there were many ways in which the blame—if one thought of it as blame—could be transferred.

He went into the kitchen, where James was chopping onions. Bach played quietly in the background, emanating from an expensive set of speakers placed in the corner of the room.

"I hope I never see her again," Neil muttered, almost to himself.

James looked up, wiping at his eyes with a piece of paper towel. "Onions," he said in explanation, and then, "You're angry."

Neil sighed. "I know I shouldn't be. Anger doesn't help."

"No," said James. "In general, no. But . . ." His chopping intensi-fied; the onions were suffering. "But there will be times when anger is the right thing to feel—the human thing, sure, but also the right thing. People talk about justified anger, don't they?"

Neil looked at his friend. "Do you ever feel that angry? Real anger?"

"About what?"

Neil waved a hand. Where would one start? "About the state of the world. Or . . ." He hesitated before continuing, "About a remark that somebody makes, or about something that somebody does." He paused. He knew that many gay people experienced hostility, hidden or overt, at some point, in spite of all the progress made in putting a stop to that. You could not change human nature by leg-islative or social fiat, and unkindness would always exist. People seemed to need an idea of the Other onto whom they could project their disappointments or fears about themselves.

"You mean, when I realise that somebody's hostile?"

"More or less."

James hesitated. "I often feel sad, rather than angry. Cruelty makes me feel that way. When I see somebody putting somebody down, or taking advantage of them, I just feel sad, really, that people can spoil things for other people when we've all got such a short time on this planet. I feel sad that people stop others from being happy." He scooped the chopped onion into a bowl. "That's that. Crying over."

James ran his hands under the cold tap. "It's odd how running water stops you crying when you've been dealing with onions." Drying his hands, he turned to Neil. "I'm going to have a glass of wine. Would you like one?"

Neil said that he would. James poured, then he raised his glass. "To Garve Point," he said.

Neil looked puzzled.

"The name of the house over there. Garve Point. A corruption of a Gaelic name, I think."

Neil lifted his glass. "Garve Point."

"Don't hesitate to tell me if you have second thoughts," said James.

Neil said he would not, but he did not think it likely.

James shook his head. "That woman. She's so . . . so spineless. Mind you, everybody's spineless. The first whiff of trouble and they fold up—and it doesn't matter who's on the casualty list." He paused. "I can't stand people like that. They're tyrants. They virtue-signal like nobody's business, but at heart they don't care about anybody but themselves. They certainly don't care whose careers they wreck." He paused. "And the way I see it, she's wrecking my friend's career."

"I'll be all right," said Neil. "But thank you, anyway."

James continued, "I'd love to push her under a bus. I'd like to . . ." He stopped himself. "Okay, that's a bit extreme. And I wouldn't do it, because then they'd suspect you. You're her victim and so you have a motive. You'd carry the can for what I did."

"I don't think I'd have the courage," said Neil. "Even if I thought she deserved it—which she doesn't. Nobody deserves to be pushed under a bus."

"If you were the midwife delivering the infant Hitler," said James. "Wouldn't you have felt justified in smothering him? That would presuppose that you knew what lay ahead, which you wouldn't, of course."

"Probably. But even then, I don't think I could."

"You might surprise yourself," said James.

He reached over to top up Neil's glass. James drank a little bit too much, thought Neil; just a little.

"Perhaps you need an avenging angel," James said. "Perhaps

you need somebody to do what you don't want to do, but needs to be done."

Neil laughed. "You?"

James winked.

"You aren't serious about revenge, are you?" Neil asked, half jokingly, but only half; people could do surprising things.

"Why not? Why should people get away with it?"

Neil shook his head. "I'm not interested in settling any scores with Henrietta."

"It would do her a power of good."

Neil shook his head again. "Maybe. But I don't think we'd land any blows."

James held up his hands. "So we take it on the chin."

Neil questioned the use of *we*. "I don't want to be rude, James, but this is my battle—not yours. This is between Henrietta and me. I really don't think you should get involved. Sorry, but there we are."

James shrugged. "All right, but it seems to me that the battle, as you call it, is over. Game, set, and match: Henrietta wins. Forget fairness. Forget truth. Any nineteen-year-old with a sense of mission can get up and accuse anybody of anything—and be believed. Great. So that's where we are. Mao's China; Stalin's Russia—here we are—same place, same mood music."

"I'm not denying any of that," said Neil. "But the point is this: you can't defeat the zeitgeist. And the truth of the matter is that liberal values have been chucked in the bin. There's no room for nuance any longer: there's the prevailing ideology and that's it. If you don't agree with the way things are, then tough luck. And there's nothing new in that, of course—if you have a sense of history. When was the last person executed for heresy in Scotland? The seventeenth century, which is not all that long ago. When did the last person lose his job because he inadvertently gave offence to somebody? Last week, probably." He paused. "Are we interested in anybody's innocence? Are we interested in what they *meant*? No. Mob justice. Quick. Unforgiving. Just as in my own case."

"Lie back and accept it?" said James. "Is that what you're saying?"

"People try to fight this thing. Have they ever succeeded? I don't think so. Sure, I could try, but I know I'd fail. The playing field isn't level—it just isn't. I could shout about fairness and so on, but is there anybody to listen? I just don't have the energy. Sorry."

James frowned. "You can't give up. You can't be so defeatist."

"But I know what the result would be. What's the point of fighting a battle that you are absolutely sure you'll lose?"

"You fight it for the next person," said James.

Neil looked down at the floor. James was right; of course he was. You had to fight the losing battle because that was the only way of protecting what needed to be protected. And yet now, faced with the need to do just that, he felt drained of moral energy.

"Maybe I will," he said. "Later. For the moment I want to get away from it."

"Because of this business with Chrissie? Is that it? I suppose I can see how you might feel you've had enough for the time being."

Neil seized at the concession. "Yes. If I can be a bit of a defeatist right now, I'll try to report for duty later—once I feel a bit better."

He looked at James. Then he said, "I don't want you to do anything. Right? I just don't. Thank you for offering, but no."

"I never offered," said James. "You might have thought that I did, but I didn't. It was all hypothetical."

"Please keep it that way," muttered Neil.

PART

Two

Nine

She was looking at him in frank appraisal, her green-grey eyes first upon his face and then the rest of him, taking everything in. Neil noticed that she seemed to be studying his hands, as if she were judging them for what they said about him. *City type; not working hands . . .* His own gaze went to her hands, which were browned by the sun, and had been used. *A countrywoman, used to digging and collecting eggs from the henhouse, and . . .*

When she spoke, her voice told him a bit more, but not too much. It was not the accent of the Western Highlands, the Gaelic softness that seemed to have all but disappeared; but it was Scottish nonetheless, with the rhythms of Glasgow, he thought, or of the hinterland behind it.

She said, "James told me you were coming. Or he told Stuart. I was over in Oban. The dentist. All that way—just for a check-up and a few words of advice about regular flossing. I thought: do I need to catch a ferry and go all the way down to Oban for that?"

He smiled. Living in a city, it was easy to take everything for granted, including dentists. It was different here. He glanced at Maddy. She was an attractive woman, with the high cheekbones that gave a face more definition. People with that look, he had always thought, *meant* something—as opposed to the rest of us, to whom life tended just to *happen*. But that, he knew, was absurd. Cheek-bones had nothing to do with character. And yet so many people looked the part.

James had told him about Stuart and Maddy, whose house lay down the track, round the corner, the closest neighbours in a place of sparse people. Stuart, who was in his early forties, had come to Mull from Perthshire, raised oysters, he said, cultivating them on flat beds in the sea-loch—an oyster rancher, as they called them. *Rancher* was a such a strange term, he had added, but that was what he was—as well as being a fisherman, on and off, who set a string of creels on the west side of the island, and provided, when he caught them, cod for the fish van in Tobermory. He took visitors out on his boat—divers, too. There were plenty of shipwrecks.

"Everybody does everything," James had said. "Or at least three things, to keep body and soul together. Maddy, his wife—she's a bit younger than he is—knits sweaters, keeps goats, and designs web-sites. She's an interesting character—very well read. You don't neces-sarily expect to find people like that living out in the blue, but there she is. She's from Glasgow originally, but she's a graduate of St. Andrews, I think. English literature, or classics, or something like that."

Now Maddy was at her doorway, and was inviting him in.

"James leaves the keys with us," she said. "I check the house for him, but you'll be there now. It's better to have somebody living in it." She wrinkled her nose. "It can get musty if it's closed up for too long."

She took him into the kitchen. A dog that had been sleeping in front of the range came up to him and nuzzled at his trouser leg. "That's Grouse," she said. "He's the laziest dog on the island. He really can't be bothered."

Grouse looked up at Neil, and then moved back to the blanket on which he had been sleeping.

"See?" said Maddy. "That's his exercise for the day. He's a complete waste of space, that dog, but we love him to bits. And he knows it. He knows we'd never fire him for failing to do the things that dogs are meant to do." She paused, and smiled. "I have a teleological view of dogs, I must admit."

She gestured to a chair. "I imagine you need something to eat after the journey. I can offer you soup . . . or soup, I suppose. There's also a bit of bread. Or a slice or two of cold lamb. That's it, I'm afraid. I've been working all morning and haven't really got round to organising lunch."

He looked at the table, where a laptop computer was surrounded by a muddle of papers.

"James told me you designed . . ."

"Websites. Yes. I'm actually qualified to do it. Most of us do all sorts of things we have no qualifications for, but I've got the piece of paper." She glanced at the table. "I build websites, but I also keep them going—service them. Mostly for whisky distilleries. They're my main customers. I look after a few down in Islay, but there are plenty of new distilleries opening all the time. Everyone wants to make whisky."

He sat down.

"I'm not particularly hungry," he said. "But a bowl of soup— if it's no trouble . . . If I'm not taking you away from something important."

"Nothing's any trouble," she said. "Nor important, for that matter. The point about here—about this place—is that nothing's particularly urgent. So we have time to do things." She paused. "You're a doctor, James said over the phone. Do you work with him?"

Neil shook his head. "He's a different sort of doctor. He's a dermatologist. We were medical students together."

"And what sort of doctor are you?"

"Public health. I've been doing a research job recently, rather than seeing patients. I monitor how people pass things on to another. Or get sick because they eat the wrong things, drink too much, and, when they aren't eating the wrong things or drinking, smoke. Or live in damp houses, because that's where we expect them to live. I teach medical students about infection and communicable diseases. Not very glamorous, I'm afraid."

She nodded. "He said that you were taking a break."

"Yes, I am. I don't think I'll go back to what I was doing. I might change jobs completely and go into general practice. Give people pills for high blood pressure and so on. Listen to their chests. Listen to what they have to say about their aches and pains. Apply the sticking plaster that we need to apply to one another to keep going."

He waited. She would ask why he was taking a break, he thought, and he would tell her. He knew that in places like this, word soon got round, but it was possible that James had already mentioned to her the reason for his leaving Edinburgh.

"I'm in disgrace. James might have told you about it."

She did not seem surprised. "He said something about your having a problem at work. He said you wanted to get away."

"But he didn't tell you what the problem was?"

She shook her head. "He didn't." She smiled. "But you say that you're in disgrace. *When, in disgrace with fortune and men's eyes . . .*"

He looked up at her. The words were familiar, but he did not know why.

"*I all alone beweep my outcast state . . .* It's a Shakespeare sonnet. I love them. I always have. It's my main thing, so to speak— Shakespeare's sonnets."

She gave him a bemused look. "I suppose you're sitting there thinking: who's this person on the west coast of Mull quoting Shakespeare's sonnets at me? I wouldn't blame you if you thought that. But I like poetry—I just do—and there are worse things to do with one's time."

"Of course. Why not? I've read a couple of the sonnets, I suppose. We did them in English at school. I didn't understand them then—or I don't remember understanding them."

"The words flow over you," she said. "They're so beautiful. You don't need to think of the meaning—in fact, I didn't for a long time. I thought they were just words—then I came to realise that they were ideas as well."

She busied herself with a pan on the range. This was the soup. As she stirred, she spoke to him over her shoulder. "James didn't say anything. And you don't have to tell me. There are plenty of people these days who seem to be in disgrace for one reason or another. Perhaps we live in shaming times."

He told her that he liked that expression. It was true, he said, about shame. "We're all meant to be ashamed about something," he said. "About who we are; about our past." He paused. "Sometimes for good reason. Our past was pretty awful, I suppose."

She reached for a soup bowl. "Some of it, yes. And I suppose we should be ashamed of those parts. But not the whole lot."

"No."

"And a lot of the time, people talk about how other people should be ashamed," she continued. "They don't start with themselves."

He thought about this, but before he could say anything Maddy continued, "I'm a Campbell, you know. My father was a Campbell, and he married a Campbell. That makes me a distilled Campbell, so to speak. And Campbells have a lot to answer for round here. It's ridiculous, but I'm not imagining it."

"The massacre of Glencoe? Rather a long time ago, wasn't it? Surely nobody thinks about that any longer."

She laughed. "You'd think that, wouldn't you? But some of these old grudges take a long time to die. Look at the way people go on about Bannockburn and various scraps with the English. They act as if the fourteenth century was but yesterday."

Neil knew what she meant. The historical animosity between the Scots and the English filled pages in every Scottish history book. There were resentments spoken and unspoken, but real enough. He sighed. "Historical hatreds are like Japanese knotweed—the roots go deep, spread out in every direction, and are difficult to eradicate. The only way of dealing with them is to allow forgetfulness to do its work. If we forget . . ." He was about to add *forgiveness,* but Maddy had something to say.

"But people don't want to forget," she interjected. "They keep reminding themselves of the past. They prefer the comfort of hatred. Liking other people—loving them—is hard, because people are not always lovable. And, if you talk down to others, you get a momentary boost yourself."

They looked at one another. Neither had expected the conversation to delve so quickly into these profound issues. For Maddy, the turn it had taken pleased her: there were few other neighbours with whom she could engage in such talk. They discussed sheep, and mussels, and the weather; their agenda was dogs and eagles and the cancellation of ferries at awkward times. They did not talk about shame and guilt and the psychology of antipathy.

"I wasn't going to ask you what happened," she said suddenly. "But you mentioned it, and now, if you don't tell me, I'll sit here and think about it and probably come up with a far more sinister explanation." She paused. "So perhaps you might like to tell me after all why you were in disgrace."

Neil told her about Tom and his misunderstanding of what he had said. He told her about Henrietta's apparent partiality and her readiness to pander to a groundless complaint. She shook her head as he spoke.

"Unbelievable. That horrid young man."

He thought of Tom, and he found that he did not think of him with any particular feeling. He was not a horrid young man; he was just the catalyst.

"It's not him," Neil said. "He was just the pretext. It's her."

"Your boss?"

"Yes."

Maddy shook her head again. "She wanted rid of you? Was that it?"

It was not that simple, he thought, but here, for this conversation, it would do.

"Possibly. There may have been other factors at work, but possibly, yes."

Maddy said that she found it hard to believe that this sort of thing could take place in a time when employees' rights were meant to be protected.

"That's what I felt," said Neil, adding, "To begin with. But then I came to realise that when it becomes political, it's a different story. Yet that's where we are now."

"And you say that you didn't say anything remotely like that? Like whatever it was you were accused of saying?"

"No, I didn't. I said that I found certain living conditions disgusting—I didn't find the *people* disgusting. I wouldn't. I don't think like that."

"So, you left?"

He nodded. "Yes. I wasn't prepared to submit to the humiliation she wanted. Why should I? I'd done nothing wrong. You don't apologise for things you haven't done."

"No. You don't."

Neil hesitated. "And there was something else. My partner had an affair. I didn't know anything about it, and then I discovered it. I felt completely let down."

Maddy winced. "One thing on top of another?"

"Yes. It wasn't good timing." He made an effort. He did not want to sound self-pitying. Chrissie was in the past. He would soon forget about her, or, rather, not worry about her. One had to become indifferent to the things you could not do anything about, unless you were prepared to let them hurt you indefinitely. "I'm all right, though. Worse things have happened."

"You had no idea?"

Neil shook his head. "None. I thought . . . well, I thought we were fine. She seemed happy—I was happy. We got on. And then she took up with an interior decorator—not that it made any difference that he was an interior decorator. But she took up with him, and that was that."

Maddy said that she could see why he was upset. "I'm very sorry to hear all this," she said.

"Thank you. But look, let's not talk about all that. People break up. They start again."

She poured soup into his bowl and passed it to him. "You'll feel better up here. Lots of people have something they need to get away from, and then they come up here and things don't seem so bad."

"I hope so," said Neil.

"Oh, it'll happen all right," Maddy assured him. "There's nothing like a remote spot to put things into perspective. People think that everything is in terminal decline, and then they come here and they suddenly find that life is a lot simpler—and less threatening—than they imagined. The sea, the hills, everything—they have an effect on you. I don't know if there's a name for it, but it exists."

"Calm? Quiet?"

"Either of those will do." She gave him an encouraging look. "I can imagine how you've been feeling."

He dipped his spoon into the soup. "Thanks. I'll be all right, though."

"I'll take you down to the house after lunch. I'll show you how to turn on the hot water system—it's very eccentric, but it does work. It helps to talk to it in Gaelic."

"Which I can't do."

"I'll tell you what to say."

They both laughed.

"May I offer you a bit of advice?" she said. "Don't do anything for the first two or three days. There's a window in the front of the house that has a window seat. Sit there and look at the sea. Doing that sets things in perspective."

"I will," he said. "I'm quite happy to look at the sea."

"The cushion on that window seat is a bit chewed," she continued. "A friend of James's came to stay a few months ago and he had this dog that chewed everything—including the window-seat cushion. You know what James is like—he's usually very mild—but he was furious. He has a bit of temper underneath it all, you know."

Neil raised an eyebrow. Moderate, patient James?

"Really?"

"Yes. I've seen him get angry with somebody. We were all having a meal with some people who live a few miles away—over towards Tobermory—and our host made an unpleasant remark. It was something intolerant, hurtful really, that James took exception to—and he, well, he looked as if he could quite easily have taken a swipe at this person. I would have thought that he could easily have resorted to physical violence—he was that angry."

Neil did not say anything. But he remembered his conversation about Henrietta with James. He had glimpsed something there that he had never seen before. James was a good loser at squash—on the rare occasions that he lost. Competitive games could bring out anger, but that had never happened, as far as he knew.

"I know James quite well," he said. "I've known him for years. I've never seen signs of a temper."

Maddy shrugged. "People are different things to different peo-

ple." She smiled at Neil. There would be so much to talk about.
"But, anyway—let's get down there so that you can get settled in.
I'll drive down in my car—you follow me in yours. Be careful,
though: the track's pretty rough. James says that he'll do something
about it, but he hasn't got round to doing it yet. One day he will, but,
until then, watch your car's suspension. Stuart has a Land Rover that
can take anything. You'll see it parked down there when he's out on
his boat."

They went outside. Grouse began to follow Maddy, but then
thought better of it and returned to his blanket by the range.

"Lazy dog," muttered Maddy. "Please forgive his bad manners."

It was still outside, and the early afternoon sun was high above
them. He heard the sea, he thought, or something that could be the sea.

"Stuart will be back later on," she said. "He's fishing this afternoon because of the weather. He keeps it on a mooring just off your
place." She corrected herself. "I mean, James's place, although it's
yours now, isn't it, for the time being."

"Yes."

"Mind you," she said, sweeping a strand of hair off her brow.
"Most of the things we have are ours just for the time being. We like
to think they're permanent, but they aren't." She paused. "Scotland,
this island, the whole world, I suppose: we're just the temporary
custodians."

"Custodians who aren't doing a particularly good job," he said.

She turned to him and smiled. "But have we ever?"

Before he could think of an answer, she pointed to a van parked
beside the house. "That's me," she said.

The van was white, or had been. Now it was streaked with mud
and with bruises on its metal where it had been bumped or scratched
and rust had got in. There was something painted on its side in large
letters that he could barely make out. Something about fish.

"It was a fish van," she said. "It belonged to a man called Donald

Mackay, who used to live in Salen. He sold fish all over the island to people who couldn't catch it themselves. He died, and I bought it from his widow, who's a primary school teacher in Tobermory. I love it, but it still smells of fish. You can't get rid of that smell, you know." She paused. "If you ever need to travel in it, you'll need to keep the windows open."

He laughed. "That's okay. I'm not fussy."

"You can't be," she said, as she moved towards the van. "Otherwise, you wouldn't be here, would you?"

He asked her why she should say that.

"Because we have to settle for what we've got," she replied, adding, "Most of the time."

I've just done that, he thought. I've settled, rather than fought back.

Ten

He saw the boat coming in later that afternoon. At first it was an indistinct black speck in the distance, rounding the headland; shortly afterwards he was able to make out more detail: the fenders attached to its sides, the spike of the radio mast, the stowed creel, and the figure of a man inside the cuddy rising from the foredeck. There was a slight swell on the sea, and the vessel, a small fishing boat of the sort popular with inshore fishermen, rose and dropped with the waves passing beneath it. A few gulls, hoping for scraps, wheeled and dipped above the wake behind the stern, before flying off, complaining noisily in their disappointment, towards the shore.

He watched as the man secured the boat to its mooring before climbing into the tethered dinghy and rowing back to the jetty only a few yards from the front of the house. As he approached, Neil made his way down to meet him. The gulls, still circling, watched him from above, and then flew off inland.

"Stuart?"

The man secured the dinghy to the jetty and then disembarked. He reached out to offer a handshake. "That's me. Welcome." He peeled a battered work cap from his head, roughly flattening down a mop of dark hair.

Neil noticed the eyes, which seemed to him to have the same brightness as he had seen in Maddy's. These were people, he decided, who were used to distant horizons—the sea, Ben More and the mountains that rose to the south-east, the offshore islands on the perimeter of this stretch of the Hebridean sea.

"No mackerel, for some reason," Stuart said. "I usually come back with a few. Not today."

They shook hands and began to walk up the path to the house.

"Maddy showed you everything?"

"She did."

"Including the hot water system?"

"Including that. I think I know what to do."

They went inside. "You'll need to keep your windows closed when you're not in," said Stuart. "You get birds coming in. And pine martens sometimes. There was a family of them a year or so ago that took up residence in the roof space. Not a good thing."

"I'll look out."

"There are mink too, nasty little creatures. I take it you're not planning to keep hens, but if you did, you'd have to be very careful. Mink are great ones for blood sports. They'll kill a whole coop of chickens for the sheer hell of it."

Neil said that he had no intention of keeping any livestock—even hens. "If they count as livestock, that is—which I imagine they don't."

Stuart laughed. "They're a bit easier than sheep—or goats. They're much easier than goats, in fact. Maddy keeps goats, you know. It's like having children. You get very caught up in their lives—and they know it. Goats are very intelligent."

"I don't want to complicate my life," said Neil. "It's bad enough..." He stopped himself. He had not intended to say that, and now he saw that Stuart was looking at him with interest, waiting for him to say more.

He would have to explain. Stuart would be talking to Maddy about it, of course, and she would tell him. "I don't really mean that.

I'm not saying that my life is a mess, or anything like that. It became a bit complicated."

Stuart looked away. Neil felt that he had embarrassed him—and he could imagine why. He was an outsider—somebody who had descended upon their rather isolated existence, bringing baggage with him. They must get a lot of that, he decided—people who were running away from something or other and thinking that they might find solace or a solution at the end of the road.

"I had a problem at work."

Stuart looked at him again. "I work for myself out here. I sometimes think how lucky I am to be in that position—especially when I hear what people have to put up with when they work with other people. It's other people who are the problem, I sometimes think."

Neil relaxed. "I don't want to burden you with it. I was accused of saying something I didn't say. It became complicated after that."

Stuart shook his head. "I don't think anybody can say anything these days—from what I read. There'll always be somebody to object to what you say."

"It seems a bit like that," Neil said.

Stuart looked at his watch. "I have to get over to Tobermory to collect something from the vet. One of Maddy's goats has mastitis. Poor girl is really uncomfortable. The vet over there is giving us something to treat it with. She's very helpful. We're lucky to have her." He paused. "I'm sorry if you've had problems. You can put them behind you now that you're here. Nobody's going to make a fuss over anything that's happened in Glasgow."

"Edinburgh, actually. I was in Edinburgh."

Stuart shrugged. "Same thing. On the mainland." He gestured vaguely towards the hillside behind. "Do you know Tobermory, by the way?"

Neil said that he had been there once when he was a student.

Stuart nodded. "It's a grand wee place. The harbour. The line of shops round the bay. All those brightly coloured houses."

"Yes, it's pretty."

"There's the Western Isles Hotel," Stuart went on. "And a bookshop. And a whisky distillery. A hardware store that still sells buckets and things that you actually need."

He glanced at his watch again. "I have to get over there. It's half an hour's drive and I need to be there before five." He hesitated. "Do you fancy a trip? We could pop into the Mishnish afterwards—that's the bar. See who's there. We'd be back by seven."

Neil looked about him. One of his cases stood unopened near the door.

"Of course, you've only just arrived," said Stuart. "Some other time. I'll take you over and show you around. Would that suit?"

"Of course," replied Neil. "But I'd like to come now, if you can give me five minutes?"

They drove up the track in Stuart's Land Rover, an ancient vehicle kept together, Neil thought, by pieces of twine and twisted wire. There were feathers and tufts of sheep's wool and the general detritus that goes with boats and farms. Stuart apologised for the mess, but added that at least it smelled better than Maddy's old fish van. "Vehicles have personal histories, don't they?" he said with a grin. "Her van has a history of fish."

There were few cars on the road to Tobermory, a single-track of tar with passing places at regular intervals, each marked with a white diamond on a post. The drivers they did encounter seemed to be known to Stuart, and waves were exchanged as they pulled in to allow the other cars to pass.

"By next Wednesday they'll know who you are," Stuart observed. "It's that sort of place. People take an interest."

Neil said, "Better than indifference."

"Oh yes," agreed Stuart. "Once I get past the Corran ferry and on the road to somewhere else—Fort William, Glasgow, or wherever, I have to remind myself not to wave at other drivers. I forget that nobody's interested over there."

"I know what you mean," said Neil.

Stuart glanced sideways. "Yet you've come here to get away. Are you sure you're going to find what it is you're looking for?"

"Do you mean privacy? I'm not sure that's what I want. Sometimes you want to get away from something that's become too much. You want to put something behind you." Neil paused. "I know it may seem a bit odd to you, but I just wanted a break."

Stuart nodded. "I can understand that." He hesitated, as if uncertain as to whether he should stray into a sensitive area. "You said you broke up with your partner?"

"Yes. She broke up with me, I suppose. She . . . Well, she went off with somebody else, and that was that. Not an unusual story. It's hardly headline news."

Stuart said that he was sorry to hear that. "I suppose that sort of thing happens often enough. Little tragedies. Little triumphs. Little things happening in everybody's lives."

Neil looked out of the window. The road was climbing now; the sea was behind them. There were other islands in the distance. The afternoon was filled with blue. "What about you?" he asked.

"Me?"

"Have you and Maddy been together long?"

For a few moments Stuart did not answer. Then he said, "Ten years. We married ten years ago, when we were both around thirty. We knew one another for a few years before that, though—since we were about twenty-six."

"That's quite a long time."

"Enough to know that we made the right decision," said Stuart.

He frowned. "Not that I meant to say anything about your decisions. But obviously that was not . . . not right for you."

"So it seems," said Neil. He tried not to sound bitter, but did not succeed.

"I'm sorry," said Stuart. "It can't be easy." He paused. "You'll find somebody else, no doubt. You must meet people in your work."

"I do."

They turned a corner. A couple of ewes, standing in the middle of the road, trotted out of the way.

"Come on, ladies," said Stuart. "They belong to Henry Wilson. He has a large farm around here. You'll meet him soon, I imagine. He drops in to see Maddy—he doesn't care about me, I suspect. If my boat sank tomorrow—with me on board—he wouldn't waste his time. He'd be there with flowers—for her."

Neil was not sure what to say.

"I'm not saying there's anything between them, of course," Stuart continued. "Maddy knows that he's soft on her. Women pick up these things. She talks about it. She calls him *my admirer*. She makes a joke of it—not to his face, of course. Henry would be very upset about that."

"I see."

There was an abrupt change of subject. "It seems strange to me," Stuart said. "You're a doctor, and we expect doctors always to be working. I know you're as much entitled to breaks as anybody else, but it still seems odd."

"I'll get back to it," said Neil. "But it's not uncommon, you know. People often have a few months between jobs, even in medicine. We're no different from anybody else."

"Of course. And I imagine that there are plenty of doctors who deserve that sort of break. Of course, you could pick up a bit of work if you wanted." Stuart looked thoughtful. "There's a GP practice that always has people filling in for a month or two. Locums. They rely on them."

He glanced at Neil expectantly.

Neil felt a momentary irritation. He wondered whether there was implicit criticism here. People sometimes regarded doctors as their property. "Perhaps. I'll see."

Stuart nodded. "This vet we're going to see," he said, "knows what she's doing. She had a job in Glasgow—a good one. She said that she did a lot of complicated surgery on dogs. People spend money on their pets—they don't on their cows and sheep. Horses, perhaps, but not farmyard animals."

"Why did she come here then?"

Stuart shrugged. "The same reason that you did, maybe. To get away. Glasgow's a big city. Not everybody likes that sort of thing. Vets are country people at heart. In a city they see indulged dogs and unfriendly cats."

"Cats are ungrateful," Neil said. "It's all on their terms, isn't it?"

Stuart nodded his agreement. "We have a cat in our barn. It lives there and we feed it, but it doesn't really like us. I think it despises me—for some reason. I tried, but obviously not hard enough. Whereas dogs—"

Neil smiled. "They signed up to something quite different— a long time ago. There's a contract between us and them. They get food and in return they do what we ask of them."

"You're probably right," Stuart said. But he had reservations. "Our dog may be an exception, of course. He does nothing."

Neil said that he had met him. "Perhaps he doesn't see the need."

"He's decadent. Some dogs just are. That's what decadence is, don't you think? Not seeing the need to do anything about any-thing." He looked at Neil. "Do you think this country's become decadent? Do you think we take it all for granted? Entertain our-selves with frippery?"

Neil said that he was not sure. "Do you think that?"

"A bit," Stuart replied. "And it depends which country you're talking about. Decadence and silliness go together, I've always thought. You only have to turn on the television set to see silliness."

Tobermory could be seen below them. Now Stuart said, "You'll like the vet."

"I'm sure I will."

"Henry doesn't."

There was a silence. Then Neil asked, "They've fallen out over something?"

"Yes, but I'm not sure what it was. People find all sorts of things to fall out over. There's no shortage. Look at the world about us. Religion, politics, land: all these things that large groups of people can fall out over. Mostly land, I suppose. That's the one. Competition for space."

"All those things—yes."

"Mind you," Stuart continued, "there are plenty of reasons to do the opposite—to fall *for* somebody rather than to fall *out* with them. As long as you're ready to do it. You have to be ready for that, don't you think? You probably aren't—not at the moment. You're probably saying to yourself that the last thing you want to do is meet somebody—or at least not just yet."

Neil looked away. He felt slightly uncomfortable with the intimacy of the conversation. "I don't know," he said. "I'll wait and see."

As they made their way down the hill behind the town, past the first neat houses, with their view across the sound, he wondered whether this might be a place where people occupied themselves with the lives of others—because there was nothing much else to do. You might be occupied with keeping sheep or fishing or making goat's cheese, but the affairs of those around you might be the savouring that kept monotony at bay.

He decided to make it clear. "At the moment," he said, "I don't want involvement. I want to be on the sidelines, if you see what I mean."

Stuart nodded sympathetically. "I understand that perfectly. It's what I am, I suppose."

Neil looked surprised. "But you've got a lot going on. Farming, and so on. Your boat. Maddy said you take divers out to shipwrecks."

"Yes, I do. And yes, there's quite a bit to keep me busy. But that doesn't mean you don't have time to think."

"Of course not."

"People imagine that farmers don't think very much. But they're wrong, you know. We get plenty of time to think. When you're out there with the sheep or cattle, or driving your tractor, you have plenty of opportunity to think. We have more time to think than people who live in cities. They rush around all the time—they don't stand still and think."

Stuart slowed the Land Rover. "That's us, over there. That's where we pick up the ointment for Maddy's goat. That's the vet's place."

They turned into a narrow driveway. An upturned boat—every house seemed to have one—occupied the space next to the garage. A sign announced the opening hours of the veterinary surgery, adding underneath, a permissive rider: *And at all other times too, depending.*

"A word of warning," said James, as he switched off the engine. "The vet, Jill, is the sort of person men fall in love with. She's a looker. Men fall for her—every one of them. I've seen it time and time again."

"And they all get rebuffed?"

James laughed. "Most of them. But she's very kind about it. She's very charming. She was involved with a pilot for a year or so. He flew on a route from Oban to the Outer Isles, but dropped in at our airfield whenever he could. Then that fizzled out." He paused. "But every man I've spoken to about her seems to have fallen under her spell. Maddy says she's a modern incarnation of Circe. How's your Homer?"

"Virtually non-existent," Neil replied. "I've heard of him. That's about it."

Stuart kept his hands on the wheel. The cooling of the engine made a ticking sound. Somewhere behind them, the river that leapt down the hill to the foreshore roared in spate; there had been rain over the previous few days.

"I've never actually read it," Stuart said. "Not the actual poem. But Maddy goes on about it, and I'll get round to doing it one of these days. I had a stab at it some years ago, but gave up." He sighed. "There's a lot of things I haven't done. Reading Homer is just one of them. Gone to Iceland. Ridden in a gondola in Venice. Travelled to Alice Springs on that train they have—the one that goes from Darwin."

"Your bucket list," said Neil.

"Yes, my bucket list. We have a lot of time to be dead. Oh, well . . . Circe had an island. Odysseus called in on his way home—he took rather a long time to get back to Ithaca, you see. She was a lengthy distraction. She was known for her expertise with potions . . ." He nodded towards the house. "Not antibiotics, of course—she concocted mixtures that would change men into swine. Prescription only. She was immensely talented. Odysseus had to persuade her to change his men back again."

"And he succeeded?"

"Yes, apparently, he did. But she rather fancied him. Well, she liked him enough to have a couple of sons by him. That was a sign, I suppose." He lowered his voice. "Maddy says that Circe represents freedom for women. That's what she stands for, and that was a big step—a big idea, until recently, that is. And men—that's us, of course—disapproved. We wanted to shut women away." He began to open the door. "Not any longer, of course—except in lots of places."

They walked towards the side entrance of the house. "Remember," said Stuart. "Remember the vet's called Jill—not Circe."

Neil grinned. "I'll try."

He thought: this is an unusual farmer. But then he had decided that Mull was an unusual island. The thought cheered him. He did not want to be bored: just because you wanted to get away from something, it did not necessarily mean that you wanted to be bored.

The vet came to the door when they rang the bell. Stuart introduced her to Neil. She looked at him, and smiled briefly. Neil felt her gaze upon him, like the touch of a hand.

"I'll get it," she said. "Give me a moment."

She disappeared into the house. Stuart turned to Neil. "See?" he said.

"I suppose I do."

"Of course you do," muttered Stuart. "Who wouldn't?"

Jill returned with a tub of ointment. "This should do the trick," she said.

"I don't want tricks," said Stuart, with a smile. "I want science."

"What do you think science is?" Jill retorted. "Tricks that happen to work."

Stuart laughed. "You should know."

Jill glanced at Neil, and then looked at her watch. "I have a call to do. I'd better go."

They returned to the Land Rover. Neil glanced back over his shoulder, and thought, *spells*.

"Well?" asked Stuart, as he started the engine. He was smiling, as if proved right about something.

"She could probably change men into swine," said Neil.

"Sometimes I regret being married," said Stuart. "Oh, there's nothing wrong with my marriage—we're very happy. But freedom has its attractions."

"I thought you said that she was bad news for men."

"Did I?"

"Yes, you implied it."

Stuart shook his head. "I don't really think that. I think she's a *temptation* for men. But she can't help that, can she? And if men are capable of resisting, then there's no problem. But men are weak, aren't they? They fly too close to the flame, you know, like moths. Then they get burned."

He began to reverse the Land Rover. "Ignore what I say, by the way. I have a tendency to be melodramatic, according to Maddy, at least."

They were on the road that led into the centre of the town. Stuart said, "We can drop into the Mishnish. Sometimes there's somebody there. At other times there isn't. Shall we investigate?"

Neil suddenly felt tired. "I'm not particularly bothered," he said.

Stuart gave him a sideways glance. "Of course. All right."

"I don't want to seem ungrateful."

"I didn't think you were." His tone had become businesslike. "We should get home and bring relief to poor Fiona. She's the goat with mastitis."

Stuart had a further errand—an order to pick up from the hardware store. After he had done that, they drove back past the vet's house. Neil gazed at the untidy yard—the upturned boat, a rusty gas cylinder, a motorcycle propped up against the garage wall. He imagined Jill in her surgery.

Stuart noticed. "You know, I love this place. I just love it."

It was a moment of mutual understanding, and yet there was a note of awkwardness to it, Neil felt: the love of one's country was not something that was usually paraded. But he wanted to say something. "Some places are easy to love," he agreed. "And I can see that this could be one."

"It is."

When they reached the farm, Neil said that he would walk down the track to his house, as he needed the exercise. He set off, looking up at the uncertain sky. The island weather was unpredictable, and could assume, and then shrug off, a mood within minutes. It started to rain, but only gently, and then it stopped, and the sun came out, bathing the fields, the hills, the sea, with gold.

E l e v e n

Over the next four days, he saw Stuart and Maddy only briefly. Stuart came down the track to launch his boat, but did not come to the house. Spotting Neil standing at a window, he waved from the shore, pointing to the fishing rod he was carrying to indicate that he was going fishing. Neil wondered whether he was being wordlessly invited to join him, but Stuart had now turned back to the task of pushing his small dinghy into the water. Then he rowed out to the larger fishing boat, bobbing on its mooring a short distance out. Neil would not have wanted to go, even had there been an invitation; he was still winding down and found that he was not keen to go anywhere. There was no pressure to go anywhere; no rush to make any decisions. Time had become different, elongated somehow, the hours moving at a slower pace than they had done in his previous existence. Perhaps people lived longer here, he thought, an island life being drawn out by the simple fact of its insularity. The surrounding sea, he decided, could make a significant difference.

Maddy brought him a fish pie in an oven dish. "All you need to do is heat this up," she said. "It'll probably do you for two days."

He thanked her. "You mustn't worry about me," he said, putting the dish down on the kitchen table.

"Oh, I wasn't worrying," she assured him. "I could tell right away that you weren't one of those men who are helpless." She gave him a playful look. "They do exist, you know—but you're not one of them."

"I had to cook at home," Neil explained. "Right from the beginning. I did my share when I was a small boy. I used to love making soup." He paused. "You must let me make you some, once I get myself organised. I have to go into Tobermory for supplies."

"There's a Co-op shop there," said Maddy. "It has just about everything, and it's usually reasonably fresh. I can give you eggs. My hens are in a good mood at the moment. And Stuart will give you fish. I hope you like mackerel."

She hesitated. It was not mackerel that she was wondering about. Then she asked, "Are you sure you're going to be all right?"

He smiled. "I'm fine—so far."

"I don't like to interfere," she said. "People have . . ." She searched for the right words. "People have their own ways of getting through life. They have their own plans."

"I suppose they do—most do them."

She gestured about the kitchen. "You're just going to stay here? You don't feel the need to . . . to do anything?" And then added, hurriedly, "Not that it's any of my business."

"I'm taking a break," said Neil. "It's not going to be for long. Just a short break."

The answer seemed to satisfy her. "And then you're going back to work?"

He wondered whether that was what was worrying her. She and Stuart were, after all, farmers, as well as being all the other things they did—website designers, knitters, makers of goat's cheese. They evidently believed in hard work, and here he was, sitting around in the kitchen, accepting fish pies made for him by others . . .

"I've always worked," he said. "And I'll be going back to work in . . ."

She waited.

"In a couple of weeks' time," he said. "A month at the most. I couldn't take a holiday of longer than a month. I'd get bored—especially here." He realised his tactlessness immediately, and tried to correct himself. "I don't mean that. Not here in particular. I meant to say that I'd get bored not working. I know that there's a lot going on here."

She helped him in his discomfort. "No, you're right. There's not much happens on the island—although everybody seems busy enough."

"I really didn't mean that."

"But I wouldn't have minded if you did. That's the whole point about living on an island. There are people who are born here, and then there are people who come here from choice. Me, for instance: I chose to live here—and not just because of Stuart. We met here—I didn't come here just because we'd got together."

"I see."

"A lot of people," she continued, "don't make that sort of choice in their lives. Life happens to them."

He said that he had been thinking about that recently—and he agreed.

"So, people who come and live here on Mull do so because they want to live their lives at a different pace—without the journey to work, the traffic, the noise, the rush." She shrugged. "Without the pressure."

He said that he could understand that.

"But if they think they won't have to work, they soon realise their mistake." She looked at him anxiously. "I wasn't talking about you, of course. Doctors work hard. Everyone knows they do. Doctors and dairy farmers. I'm glad that I'm not a dairy farmer. The goats are much easier, particularly if you stop milking them. I don't make cheese all the year round. I make very little at other times, and so I let them dry up." She sighed. "Stuart wonders why I bother to keep them. I suppose it's because I like having them round the place. And I think they feel the same about me—oddly enough."

She noticed the book he had left open on the kitchen table. "I can't resist squinting at the books other people are reading. Is that rude, do you think?"

"I wouldn't have thought so. As long as you don't read over their shoulders. That might make them feel uncomfortable."

She laughed. "And looking at other people's bookshelves? What's the etiquette there? Can you take a look at what's there without seeming to be too nosy? I must admit—I can't resist."

His answer absolved her. "You can, I think."

"And draw conclusions?"

He said that he thought that conclusions would be inevitable. "Most people's shelves tell you all you need to know about them."

She was gazing at his book.

"That's *A Brief History of the Smile*."

"Interesting?"

"Yes. Smiles are not as simple as we think they are." He picked up the book and showed her an illustration of the Cheshire cat, smiling from its tree. "The Cheshire cat smile, for instance . . . what do you make of that?"

She studied the picture briefly. "Cats don't do smiles. Dogs do—not cats." She examined the picture again. "That's a threatening smile."

"Exactly. Also, a bit smug?"

She nodded. "Plenty of smiles are smug, aren't they? You sometimes see people smiling to themselves. They may be thinking of something amusing, but just as often it's because they're pleased with themselves. That sort of smile says: *I'm really rather clever.* Or, *nothing wrong with me.*"

He was intrigued by the thought of dogs smiling. "Do dogs smile? Maybe they do."

"Oh, they do," she said. "Particularly working dogs—the various collies. They have a special sort of grin. The skin at the side of their mouths flops about and you see their teeth exposed in a perfect smile. They're smiling to please us. It's a grin, really. They're saying, *I know I'm only a dog, but I'm really very keen to please. Any sheep to move? I'm the dog for that.* That's what that smile says."

Neil laughed. "Sentiments that no self-respecting cat would express?" Then, after a moment's thought, he added, "Your dog, Grouse—"

Maddy shook her head. "Grouse doesn't smile. He has a lugubrious look to him—a look of resignation, I suppose. Yes, resignation's probably what he feels most of the time. He doesn't see the point of doing anything very much."

Neil replaced the book on the table. "Why do photographers tell people to smile?" he asked. "They all do, don't they? Anybody who takes a photograph of somebody else automatically says, 'Smile please!' Why?"

Maddy replied by saying that she thought it was one of those meaningless things that people said. But then she added, "I suppose they want people to look their best, *Smile, please* probably also stands in for *Straighten your hair* or *Don't slouch so much*, or something like that."

Neil thought it was about putting a brave face on for the world. "It's a statement of belief—a clutching at straws. The world is a pretty difficult place, but, look, I'm smiling, in spite of it all. That's what photographic smiles are all about." He paused. "What's the archetypical insincere smile? The real gold standard smile that doesn't mean it?"

She shrugged. "The Cheshire cat?"

That was not the answer. "Cabin crew in aeroplanes," Neil said. "They smile as you come into the plane. Broad smiles—not only in their photographs in airline advertisements, but in real life. They smile, but underneath it they're probably at the end of their tether. They're tired. It's the second flight of the day. Their feet hurt. They want to get home, and they have to pretend that they're really pleased to see you and they're looking forward to helping you to fit your bags into the overhead lockers and showing you the emergency exits, and so on. But they've been told to smile because the airline wants you to feel that the whole uncomfortable experience of being carried through the air in a metal tube while the back of your seat is being kicked by an ill-behaved child is a positive one."

Maddy laughed. "You don't like flying?"

"I don't mind it," said Neil. "But I don't think it's anything to smile about. And if airline staff didn't smile, I'd sympathise. In fact, I might even have greater confidence in an airline that didn't present a smiling face to the world. Serious Air might be a good name for an airline. Reliable. Trustworthy. Focused on proper maintenance of its fleet—and so on."

She moved over towards the kitchen window and looked over to the bay outside. "It's a very high tide," she remarked. She turned to him. "You met the vet?"

"Yes."

She seemed to be waiting for something. Neil thought she looked bemused.

"And?" she said.

"She gave Stuart the stuff for your goat."

She nodded. "She's very helpful. What did you think?"

"Of her?"

Maddy nodded. "Yes."

It was clear to Neil that there was a point to this questioning, and he felt a momentary annoyance. Was he being set up? He would make it clear he would appear indifferent. He did not want any interference in his social life—if he was going to have one on this island, which he was not sure about anyway.

"I imagine that she has to be tough. She has to deal with farmers, and you have to know what you're doing, I would have thought, if you have to inoculate cattle and deal with lambing and so on."

"Oh, she's pretty good at all that," said Maddy, adding, "It's one of the reasons I like her. She has a way with animals, obviously, and also . . ."

She left the sentence unfinished.

"I should put the fish pie in the fridge," Neil said. It was an obvious change of subject, and Maddy sensed that. She looked away apologetically.

"And I should get back to the house," she said. "I have a long list of things to do."

"I don't," said Neil, and laughed. But then he apologised. "That sounded tactless. You have all your chores to get on with, while I'm doing nothing in particular."

"I expect," she said, "that you'll make yourself busy enough."

"Probably. I might catch some mackerel—if Stuart leaves any for me." He pointed to the fridge. "I'll bring your dish back tomorrow."

She said that he did not have to worry. "James returns them sooner or later. We seem to share kitchen things. I've got a potato masher I've been meaning to get back to this kitchen. And you've got my garlic press, I think—somewhere or other." She paused, glancing at the shelves. "That's what we do on this island. We take a pretty communal view of things." She waved a hand carelessly. "I recognise so many things in other people's houses—and they in mine, of course."

"Mutual support."

Maddy's voice expressed reservation. "Some of the time. There are occasions on which incivility breaks out. This is Scotland, after all, and we have a long tradition of arguing with one another. But we don't like to see people falling by the wayside. We have a sense of community, I think—or at least I fondly believe that."

Neil hesitated. That Scotland of comity and sedate politeness— had it ever really existed? "We spend a lot of time at each other's throats these days. Just like the French. The Americans. You name it. It's all division now, isn't it? My American friends say that nobody talks to one another any longer across party divides. There's a great chasm in their country. There are no shared goals."

She shook her head. "I've read about that."

"It's everywhere," he said. "Even Sweden, which we used to hold up as an example of social cohesion. No longer, apparently."

"Like a civil war?"

"A bit. There are no opposing armies lined up—well, not armed ones, as on a battlefield, but they're there, I suppose, sniping at one another in other ways."

She was staring at him. "Is that what happened to you?" she asked.

"Yes," he said. "In a way. I'm a pretty minor casualty—I resigned because I was being used in other battles."

"I'm very sorry." She sighed. "I find it hard to believe that these things are happening in this country."

He shrugged. "I like the word *zeitgeist*. It explains a lot. The zeitgeist at the moment is one of suspicion and hostility. We've stopped liking one another, I think. We used to be tolerant. We used to like not only others, but ourselves. That's changed, I'm afraid. All we hear about now is anger. Everybody's angry with everybody else."

She looked surprised. "Do you really think so?"

He did.

"So, what now?" she asked.

"I suppose that we need to try to get back some of the things we've lost: courtesy, listening to the other point of view, helping one another, accepting that people may have different ideas of the good; accepting, too, that people may be flawed but not entirely wicked."

She looked doubtful. "Doesn't that sound rather like a lost Eden?"

Neil paused before answering her. "We had a history teacher at school," he said. "He was called Mr. A. Peebles. We never found out what the A stood for—he was always referred to simply as Mr. A. Peebles. Anything else would have seemed, well, I suppose, disrespectful. We liked him. We couldn't stand some of the teachers, but Mr. A. Peebles was everybody's favourite."

"Miss Hamilton," Maddy muttered. "She was as thin as a rake, and she wore 4711 Eau de Cologne. It followed her through the corridors. She was ours. We loved her. She gave every girl in the class a bar of chocolate on her birthday. She never gave any to the boys— she said that boys could look after themselves. And we accepted that—as did the boys."

"Mr. A. Peebles wouldn't have approved of that," said Neil. "He was scrupulously fair. But the reason I mention him is not because he was so popular, but because he talked about civilisation in his history lessons. He said that there was such a thing as civilisation; he said this even when the word had passed out of favour—become something to be ashamed of. He said that we had to have a concept of civilisation—something we believed in—or life would become impossible. He used to go on about Thomas Hobbes and about how life could become nasty, brutish, and short. We were a sort of Greek chorus when he said that. We chanted *nasty, brutal, and short*. He didn't mind. Anyway, he said that if you didn't believe in something—some sort of ideal—then you wouldn't have any shared culture, and life in society simply wouldn't work. He said that we needed people to do the important jobs—looking after people, making sure that things worked—but that such people needed to have a reason to do what they did. Getting paid wasn't enough: people needed to believe in the value of what they were doing. If we stopped believing in value, then things would fall apart."

" 'Dover Beach,' " said Maddy. "Mr. A. Peebles knew 'Dover Beach.' I bet he did."

She waited for a moment before explaining, "Matthew Arnold's poem. I love it—it's at the heart of everything."

"I've never—" Matthew began, but was interrupted by his phone. Maddy had to go; she said he should take the call.

"We can discuss 'Dover Beach' some other time," she said, moving towards the kitchen door. "It was published over one hundred and fifty years ago, and can wait. Take the call."

She opened the door. The light came in, and the sound of arguing gulls. Neil answered his phone. It was James.

James said, "I didn't want to breathe down your neck, but I've been wondering how you've been getting on."

Neil reassured him that not only was his call not intrusive—it was welcome. "I've been meaning to get in touch with you," he said. "Everything's perfect: place, house, people. The lot."

James sounded relieved. "Maddy phoned a day or two ago. She said you seemed to be settling in, but I've been worrying about the hot water system. Have you managed to get a bath out of it?"

"I've encountered more efficient systems," Neil replied. "But Maddy taught me how to deal with it, and I'm coping. It's all down to how you hold the switch."

"Exactly."

"And I've mastered it. And the window in the bedroom that you have to—"

"Push to the side when you open it," James prompted. "Yes, that can play up a bit." He paused. "Apart from that?"

"It's all fine," said Neil. "And I'm really grateful. I like it here."

There was a brief silence. Then James continued, "Would you mind if I pitched up for a week? I have to take ten days' holiday before the end of the month, or I lose them. I thought I'd come up and paint a couple of the rooms—and do one or two other things."

Neil did not hesitate. "Of course I don't mind." And then he added, "It's your house, after all. And if you'd prefer it to yourself, I could always—"

James cut him short. There would be no question of Neil's moving out: James would take the spare room and he could stay where he was. There was plenty of room.

Down the line, Neil heard the faint sound of a radio—a news broadcast. It reminded him that he had not listened to the news nor read a paper since he arrived. There was no television set in the house and the radio in the kitchen appeared not to work. He had not bothered with emails since he left Edinburgh, and he imagined that they would be stacking up in his inbox. He knew he had to deal with them eventually; but that world seemed a long way away— that world of anxiety and issues, signalling its presence through the ether, and he felt it could wait for the moment. He had no immediate professional responsibilities, and that gave him a heady sense of freedom. This was the first time since he had qualified that he had been free of the feeling that he should be doing something—attending to a patient, reading a medical journal, keeping himself up to date with developments in public health: he had none of this to do, and it was a liberating feeling.

"There's something I wanted to tell you," James said. "I wasn't sure if I should. But I thought that you might want to know."

Neil knew immediately that this was about Chrissie. He waited for James to continue.

"I played squash with one of your colleagues—sorry, former colleagues—Alan. The toxicologist."

"Alan Barton?"

"Yes. He's a good player. Better than I am. He beat me decisively."

Neil laughed. "That'll be good for you, don't you think?"

"In moderation," said James. "He had some news, though."

"About Chrissie?"

Neil thought that perhaps James had not expected him to guess—as he now sounded slightly surprised. "Yes, actually it was. He said that she's getting a full-time post. A permanent one." He paused, and then added, "Now that you've gone."

It took Neil a moment or two to deal with this information. *Now that you've gone*, which meant that Chrissie was getting his job. The institute operated under a tight budget, and there was no money for new jobs. If Chrissie had been appointed to a full-time post, then it was effectively to his job.

Neil closed his eyes. He felt empty inside. Eventually he said, "She must be pleased."

James did not reply immediately. "She's been allocated your old office—and your teaching commitments." He paused. "They moved quickly—with lightning speed, in fact."

"Yes, I suppose they needed somebody straight away, and Chrissie was available."

"Unless it was all planned a little earlier than we think," said James.

There was a short silence. Then Neil said, "Do you mean the whole thing was planned to end this way? The complaint? My suspension?" It seemed impossible, and yet this was not the first time he had entertained the possibility. The trouble with conspiracies, he thought, is that nobody wants to be thought paranoid, and so conspirators get away with it. Yet there must be at least some conspiracies that are not the product of the undue suspicions of others.

James was cautious. "I wondered. You know how you never want to be accused of seeing things that aren't there? Well, I didn't want to make you do that. But then, Alan Barton was prepared to go there."

Neil waited.

"I'm not saying I endorse any of this," James said. "I don't have any evidence, but if you put two and two together, and if you believe what Alan said—"

"What exactly did he say?" Neil interjected.

"He said that there was a departmental meeting a day or two ago. He said that Chrissie was there—it was her first time as a full-time member of staff—and that she and Henrietta were very pally-pally. Sweetness and light—lots of it."

Neil considered this. It was not much to go on: departmental meetings were sometimes like that, with everybody agreeing about everything for some reason.

"Apparently, she sat there nodding at everything Henrietta said. There was no doubt in Alan's mind that she was firmly in that camp: tent pitched, fortifications dug, the works."

Neil said that he did not think one could draw too many conclusions from that. "People sometimes agree," he said. "Even in academia."

James was amused. "Yes, but . . . Well, there's something else. Alan said that he happened to leave the building late that night—he was working on a report. He had had to park his car in an unusual place that day because somebody had taken his parking space— you know how people do that. It's a clinical sign of psychopathy, I think—taking somebody else's parking place. It shows a complete disregard for the norms of civilised society. Wars have started on lesser pretexts."

James had a tendency to theatrical overstatement. Neil smiled. But then he realised that James was right: wars started over territory— a parking place was a token of something much bigger: a province, a country—and the complaints of the usurped driver could be every bit as clamorous as those with a larger cause.

"Alan said that since his car was parked round the back, he took a short cut across that bit of lawn. And from there, you can see into Henrietta's office, especially if her light's on—which, as it happened, it was. He saw that Chrissie was in the room with her. They were drinking wine. Alan saw the glasses. They were sitting together on that sofa she has in her office—drinking wine. Two big pals—thick as thieves."

Neil said nothing.

"I'm not saying that people can't sit about in their office and drink wine," James went on. "It's just that Alan said the thought crossed his mind that they were . . ." He broke off.

Neil said, "They were what?"

"This is Alan, not me," said James. "He thought they were celebrating."

Neil made an effort. "Well, Chrissie will be pleased to get a full-time job. And why not? Perhaps it's not unreasonable for her to celebrate with Henrietta."

"Oh, come on," said James. "I know you're a nice guy, but there are limits. Alan's not the sort to invent things. If he smells a rat, then there's a rat."

"Possibly."

James became heated. "The fact of the matter, Neil, is that you've been shafted."

Neil did not reply immediately. He was not sure that he wanted to whip himself up into a state of indignation. People did things like this to other people, and if what James and Alan said was true, then he was the victim of a tawdry plot at worst, or a simple injustice at best. But he was not going to play the victim. He would ignore the whole thing and get on with his life, doing whatever it was that he would decide to do next. A chapter in his life had ended, and he would embark upon another.

"Let's talk about it when you're up," he said to James.

They ended their conversation.

Neil went outside, thinking he might go for a walk, but the rain had come on, veils of white drifting in from the Atlantic, and so he went back inside. Before he closed the door, he looked out over the sea, the surface of which was flat—an oily sea, he thought. He could see the effect of the rain on the water—the circles, the patches of darkness. A seal's head bobbed with the swell, and then disappeared. There was the smell of seaweed, that iodine smell, the tangle. He turned round and shut out the sea. The kitchen was warm, heated by the range cooker in which he had kindled and nursed a fire. This room, small, informal, warm, was the cocoon, the refuge he had been looking for.

What James had said came back to him, each word the prick of a needle, stoking the anger he felt over what had been done to him. He had reason for resentment, he realised, but he found himself wondering why James should still sound so outraged over Chrissie's behaviour. If it was true—and he did not want to reach that conclusion—that she had been in some way complicit in his suspension, hoping that it would lead to his dismissal, then there would not be words enough to describe the betrayal. But the person who should feel the full impact of that was him, not James, who was not directly involved. It was understandable that a person might feel angered by the sight of his friend being mistreated, but James's reaction seemed to be going beyond that. Why should James feel so intensely about all this?

It suddenly occurred to him that he had missed something that should have been obvious. James had spoken to him about his feelings for somebody who could not return them. He had made that guarded confession about impossible love, and now, in a moment that was as unexpected as it was unnerving, it occurred to him that the person to whom James had been referring might have been him. An indirect declaration might be missed by those to whom it is made, but it may still be a declaration. *James has been in love with me.* No, he can't have been. James is just my friend: James, my partner on the squash court, my classmate from medical school, just James . . .

He sat down and tried to order his thoughts. He was not put out by this. It was true that he did not think of James in that way, but that did not make him dismissive of such feelings—why should he be? It could be awkward if he had to spell it out to James that his feelings could not be reciprocated—but then James knew that, judging from what he had already said. Yet it was unlikely to come to that—he had known James for a long time, and there had never been an occasion when that had been an issue. They were platonic friends, and it had never been necessary to deal with the boundaries of that friendship. If James felt otherwise, then it was entirely feasible that might trigger real animosity towards Henrietta. James was loyal, and if he saw his friend—his close friend—being victimised, it would not be surprising were he to show his anger.

He reminded himself: James on very rare occasions could overreact. He had once said on the squash court, when James had upbraided himself loudly for missing a shot, "You know something: you could easily lose it."

James had laughed. "Sure," he said. "Easily." Then he added, "Lose what? The game?"

"No. It."

James shrugged.

"You need to be careful," Neil said.

PART

Three

Twelve

James had said that he would arrive five days later, which would be that Friday. On Wednesday, Maddy walked down to the house to ask him whether he would like to come up to the farmhouse for dinner that evening. She and Stuart were having a couple of people in for a meal, and there would be room for him—if he had nothing else on.

"I'm going nowhere," he said. There was no self-pity in the remark—it was purely factual.

"I know that," said Maddy. "But it's a bit rude, don't you think, to imply that somebody has absolutely *nowhere* to go?"

Neil smiled. "Very tactful," he said. He remembered the friend in Edinburgh with whom he occasionally had lunch. When he telephoned to see if he was free, there was always a pause to allow for a notional consultation of the diary. But there was never anything in the diary—Neil knew that because he had once seen it, and the pages were virginal.

He told Maddy about this. "I always knew he could make it," he said. "The diary was a matter of pride. None of us likes to think there's nothing happening in our lives." He paused. "Except, that's the case with me—currently."

She grinned. "Then you can come?"

"Of course I can."

Maddy was pleased. "We have one of the teachers from the high school. She's retiring this year and going to live in Ireland. You'll like her. And then Jill. You met her, of course—the vet."

There was a brief silence. He felt Maddy's eyes upon him.

His voice was even. He was pleased, but he did not want to make his pleasure obvious. "Good," he said. "I'll enjoy that."

Maddy was still watching him. "Fish," she said. "It'll be more of that fish pie I gave you. It's my go-to recipe."

"Good," he said. "I'll enjoy that too."

"I should be more adventurous in the kitchen," she said, almost wistfully. "But if I find something that works, I make the most of it." She gave him a quizzical look. "What about you? Do you have . . . what do they call it? A signature dish?"

He replied without thinking. "French onion soup. I know how to make that."

"Onions," she said.

"It's not that simple."

"And cheese."

He smiled. "Once again, there's more to it than that."

She left. He looked at his watch. It was already twelve, and he had done very little with the day. He had gone down to the shore earlier that morning and had moved a tangle of rope washed up by the tide. He had examined a large jellyfish lying on the sand, its trailing tentacles stretched out like lace. There was a beauty of design in it, even in its stranded, decaying state. It was a thing of curves, of roundness, like a little planet, in a way. Suspended in the water, it would have seemed perfectly at home, a creature expertly designed to be there, moving with slow contractions, like a languorous swimmer in no hurry to reach any shore. He poked at it with a stick, at the glutinous blue-white flesh, if flesh was what it was. It was jelly, of course—something halfway between water and flesh, and there was no brain. That was the extraordinary thing, he thought: this creature had no brain, and therefore could have no sense of being. Most other creatures experienced life—this one, for all its beauty, simply *was*.

He had looked out over the bay, across the stretch of sea-loch. At the mouth of the loch there were several outcrops of rock lining the channel into open water. A cormorant sat sentry-like on one of these, its wings spread out to dry in the sun. In the distance, he could make out the shape of Coll, the nearest island to the west. It was a strip of hills interrupting the horizon, with the sea a blue line at either end of it. The day was clear enough to make out the shape of the islands to the north—of the Cuillin, the high range of mountains on Skye, the backdrop to the Small Isles, to Rhum, Muck, and Eigg, that lay protectively before them. These were like sweeps of thin watercolour, attenuated to the point where they faded into the sky above, which was only slightly lighter in its colour. He stood unmoving, watching the slow progress of a fishing boat making its way north, the white trail of its wake stretching out like a furrow ploughed in the wide blue plain that was the sea.

He had spent almost two hours down by the shore, enough time to see the encroachment of the tide, which was at springs and would soon touch the line of dried seaweed that identified an earlier high-water mark. Now, in the kitchen, at noon, he decided to read; he would deal a bit later with the email correspondence that he had been putting off. There would be nothing of much importance, but he was sure there were some that would need a reply sooner rather than later. In an electronic age it was possible to walk away, but only if one were utterly determined, and only if one no longer cared, which was not the case with Neil. Already he was beginning to feel that he should go back, that this retreat was an indulgence. He had been given an expensive medical training and he should use it. He could not at this stage take a gap year, like some carefree school-leaver heading off to Thailand. His freedom, it seemed, would be measured in weeks, and, even then, not in many of those.

He thought of his inbox, with its relentless tallying of unread messages into a reproachful figure at the bottom of the column. Several of these were from people who were unaware of his resignation and who assumed he was still in post. He would forward these to Chrissie, because they were really for her now. He would say nothing, he thought, beyond *for your attention, I think*. No, he would add, *I hope all's well with you*, which at least paid service to the conventions of courtesy. He would resist the temptation to add anything to that, and he decided there was nothing more to say, anyway.

He walked up to the farmhouse, skirting the patches of mud on the unpaved track. From a field to his right, on land that belonged to the neighbouring farm rather than to Stuart, a small herd of Highland cattle watched him suspiciously. They were troubled by midges, and with movements of the head they used their unlikely fringes of dishevelled auburn hair to dispel the clouds of tiny stinging insects. He was grateful for the fence that stood between him and them: they had calves with them, and could be fiercely protective of their offspring. An unfortunate hiker, the week before, had been trampled near Spean Bridge, and had only survived because a dog had drawn the cattle off. These cattle watching him now, he thought, would be the property of the farmer who had been said to be on bad terms with Jill. Vets and farmers did not always see eye to eye, Stuart had said to him.

He was the first to arrive.

"We'll eat in the kitchen," Maddy said, as she welcomed him. "We have a dining room, but it's used for other things—rather as people used to keep coal in the bath."

"Did they really do that?" asked Neil. "I know it was a standing joke, but I don't think it ever happened that way. The people who would keep coal in the bath were not the sort of people who had a proper bath anyway. It was one of those jokes that made fun of the working class."

"They had tin tubs, didn't they?"

"Yes," said Neil. "The tin tub was filled with water from the kettle, and then people had their bath in front of the fire or the kitchen range. Water was poured over them from a tall jug. And then plumbing changed all that."

Maddy nodded. "Yes. And with it I think a great deal of intimacy disappeared. And connection."

"Connection?"

"People would call it bonding today. You bonded with people who poured warm water over your head while you were sitting in a tin tub. You also shared a bedroom, and, as often or not, a bed. Take this house, for example: the family who lived here before Stuart's parents had two bedrooms between eight of them. The parents had a bed to themselves, but it wasn't very wide. The two youngest children slept on mattresses on the floor of their parents' room; the other four children shared two beds in a smaller room. They shared until they were twelve or so, irrespective of whether it was brothers or sisters—after that, sisters could share a bed until they left home, and brothers could share with brothers. Having your own bed was an unimaginable luxury to many. Having your own room was something only to be dreamed of." She stopped. Her voice was serious. "I don't think we should romanticise the past. This place—all of Scotland really—was very poor. We had an uphill battle because we were surrounded by more urbane, more ruthless, more ambitious people. Poor Scotland couldn't compete."

Neil glanced out of the window, at the hillside rising up behind the house. The soil was thin here, and hard to work. Outcrops of rock arose like small islands in a sea of green; clusters of gorse and whin encroached on the grazing on which the sheep and cattle depended; farming required flexibility and resourcefulness. It was a landscape in which poverty and exile had stalked for centuries. And yet the people who lived here had loved it with a passion that they never lost—even in enforced exile overseas—on the prairies of Canada and the United Sates, on the plains of Victoria or New South Wales.

Maddy followed his gaze. "The children who were brought up in this house only a few generations ago had very little, you know. I found a picture of them, taken out the back there, near where that tractor's parked, probably in the nineteen-twenties. They were flanking their parents, who were occupying two hard-backed chairs and were looking straight into the camera lens, as if eager to tell us something. Perhaps they imagined that a century later I would be examining the photograph and wondering about their lives. Of course, they're all dead. When I first saw the photograph, I was struck by one of the boys. He must have been about ten or eleven, and what made me notice him was he had no boots. Many children didn't. Families were too poor. And they walked to school, some-times for miles, every day, in their bare feet, or, if they did have a pair of boots, in footwear that was hardly up to keeping the elements out—ancient shoes handed down from sibling to sibling and getting shabbier with every new owner."

"And they died," Neil mused. "So many of them died so young."

Maddy shook her head. "They did."

"I read somewhere about parish boots," said Neil. "Poor fami-lies could claim boots on the parish, couldn't they?"

"Yes, if the parish had the funds. They were specially marked so that pawnbrokers could recognise them and would refuse to take them as security for loans. They had a special pattern of studs on the heels that singled them out." Maddy paused. "Some children were ashamed of the fact that they wore parish boots. Can you imagine today's little fashion victims wearing parish sneakers?"

They heard a vehicle outside.

"Jill," said Maddy. "That's her."

Neil felt his stomach tighten.

Stuart had been unblocking the guttering on an outbuilding and they were already seated around the kitchen table, a glass of wine before them, when he came in. He washed his hands in the sink, drying them on a tea towel hanging in front of the range.

Maddy upbraided him. "That," she said reprovingly, "is for crockery—not hands." She glanced at Jill. "Cross infection—"

Jill smiled. "Germs are good for us," she said, adding, "Within reason."

Stuart thanked her. "See?" he said. "A few germs here and there—"

"Not all germs," Jill interjected.

"*E. coli,*" muttered the other guest, Maureen. She was a small, grey-haired woman, who would have stood out in any group as a teacher nearing retirement. "They go on about that, don't they? You don't want to come up against *E. coli,* I'm told."

"Children are walking reservoirs of infection, aren't they, Maureen?" Stuart said, with a grin. "You must be exposed to everything in the school."

"Teachers have excellent immune systems," Jill said. "For precisely that reason. They get exposed to the lot—every day."

Maddy was businesslike. "We're going to have goat's cheese soufflé to begin with. Everybody all right with that?"

"Perfect," said Jill. "I've had your soufflés before, Maddy. You're the soufflé queen."

"I try," said Maddy. "I use a Delia Smith recipe for smoked fish soufflé, but use goat's cheese instead of fish. It seems to work."

"Delia never goes wrong," said Maureen. "She's infallible. Like the Pope."

"Is he still infallible?" asked Stuart. "I thought that they'd given up on that."

Maureen said that she thought the idea still existed, but was not specifically invoked.

"Imagine being the Pope," Stuart said. "Imagine realising you've got something wrong. You couldn't correct yourself without undermining your infallibility. It could be awkward."

"It's very hard to imagine being the Pope," said Maureen. "Especially if you're a woman."

Stuart smiled. "That'll come," he said. "Have patience. There'll be women priests in the Catholic Church in ten years' time. There will have to be. They're running out of young men to train in seminaries. In Scotland they have a handful in training at the moment. Eight or nine, something like that."

Jill said, "There'll be very few male vets in ten years' time. Entry classes at the vet schools are almost entirely women now."

Neil wondered why that should be. "Is that because women are more sympathetic to animals?"

Jill shrugged. "Perhaps. But medicine's going that way too, isn't it?"

"And law," Stuart suggested. "I don't know what the boys are going to do."

"They've had it all their way for a long time," said Maureen. "And girls work harder at school, I can tell you. They get better results, and so they get the places at university."

Neil glanced at Jill. Stuart had been right: there was something about her—a presence, although that was not quite the right word. Perhaps you could not put these things into words, he thought; the

appeal of people like her was beyond the reach of words. She intercepted his glance, and he looked away quickly, embarrassed. She
must be used to that, he said to himself; somebody like her would get
that every day, all the time: men looking at her. She was beautiful—
it was as simple as that. You did not need words to describe something like beauty—all you needed was to open your eyes to it. It
was there; you saw it; you felt it somewhere deep down within you.
And then you had a great deal of popular terminology at your disposal, with the word *smitten* at the head of the list.

His eye fell on her wrist. She was wearing one of those thin
black bangles that people picked up abroad—woven from elephant
hair, or whatever. Ethnic jewellery. Hers had small beads worked
into it at intervals, perhaps signifying something that might have
been explained by the seller in a market in Kenya or somewhere
like that. Sometimes these things bore a message that was destined
for a recipient—a message of love, or loyalty, or something of that
nature.

He saw that her watch was small and feminine, but that it had
a functional leather strap that was rather too big for it. That was
a practical matter, he thought, as she would presumably have to
remove that for when she was performing surgery or helping a ewe
give birth. He imagined her in the field with her patients—did vets
call them that?—with an anxious farmer standing by, waiting for
the verdict on an ailing cow or a breeding sheep down on its knees
with that foot-rot or whatever it was that made their legs buckle. He
always felt sorry for sheep he saw in that condition, trying to graze
with their front legs in that position.

He looked away, but not before he saw that she had smiled at
him, and he could see in her eyes that she was responding to him.
It was a shy smile, but there was an undeniable warmth to it. He
wondered whether his interest was so obvious—and decided that
it must be. We give signals to other people all the time; signs that

might be undetectable, because much of the time we were not looking for them.

Stuart had begun a story about something that had happened in
Tobermory. Neil missed the beginning of it, as he was thinking of
Jill. Jill, though, picked it up, and added an opinion. Maureen nodded. She knew the people involved, and it had all happened before—
many times. "Those people are like that," she said. "They just are."

Maddy had been stirring soup at the range. She turned round
and said to Neil, "Island talk."

Neil said, "Don't worry about me."

"If you met these people," Maureen said to him, "you'd appre-
ciate what we're talking about. That young man is exactly like his
father—exactly. Don't you agree, Stuart?"

Stuart did. "The father was worse, though. You know, he used to
like sitting by the road after he'd been chucked out of the pub. He'd
sit there and look up at the sky—a picture of innocence. Everybody
knew, though, that he had pinched two outboards from boats over
at Lochaline. He took them down to Oban to sell them down there.
Everybody knew what was going on."

"I can believe it," said Maureen. "I taught the boy. I met the
father a few times. I wouldn't trust him an inch."

"Most people on the island are very honest," Jill said to Neil.
"They really are. It's just that particular family—and one or two
others."

"The father, Bobby, was sitting by the road one day," Stuart said,
"when Henry Wilson drove past. He was in a hurry to catch the
Craignure ferry, but he wasn't going fast, because he'd just turned
the corner. Anyway, he felt a bump and he wondered whether he'd
hit a small animal, maybe a lamb. But he hadn't, you know. He'd run
over Bobby's foot."

Jill began to smile, but checked herself.

"It really happened," said Stuart. "He was drunk, and so he

didn't feel a thing. No damage was done, I gather—just a bruise that he must have noticed the following day, when he sobered up."

Maddy laughed. "Poor man."

"Poor man?" exclaimed Stuart.

"He's probably doing his best," said Maddy.

"Maddy is charity itself," Stuart said. He looked at her with fondness.

Maureen remembered something. "There's a wonderful story about how he was out fishing with some friend of his—Gordon Watson, I think it may have been. Gordon always felt a bit sorry for Bobby and would take him out with him when he went to check his creels. They were out off Maclean's Nose once—they'd been out all day and were having something to eat on the deck before coming back to Tobermory. Bobby has false teeth—bad diet as a young man, I suppose. He had something stuck in the upper set and so he put them to soak in a cup of water and left that in the wheelhouse. Gordon didn't see this, and he decided to clear up. He noticed water in the mug and chucked it out over the side. Bobby's dentures went with it. Forty feet of water, apparently."

They laughed, but Maddy said, "Poor Bobby."

"Life is full of misfortune," Maureen added with a sigh.

This seemed to bring silence—a moment of reflection, perhaps, during which they contemplated the ways in which things could go wrong.

The conversation wandered. After a start, in which Neil held back, feeling himself a stranger in this gathering of people who knew one another well, he found himself participating in the exchange of stories. Maureen asked about his work. Could the plague ever return? Was malaria moving north? Anything could happen, Neil said, but she should not worry too much, living on Mull. "It would be different if you were in Marseilles," he said.

Jill smiled at that. "But north is becoming more south," she said.

"Ticks," interjected Maddy. "Ticks are on the move."

Jill said that everyone should inspect themselves after going any-where near grass or bracken.

"You must have to be careful in your job," said Maddy. She shud-dered. "Going out into the fields to see cows and sheep. These ticks are so small, aren't they? Microscopic—you might never notice them, and then—"

"Lyme disease," said Stuart.

"Any of us could get anything," Neil said. "It doesn't help to brood on it." He looked at Jill. He wanted to say something to her, but he was uncertain as to what it might be. He reached a decision. "Do you mostly look after farm animals?"

"Jill does everything," Stuart said.

"Cats and dogs in the morning," Jill said. "Cows and sheep afterwards—unless it's urgent. And horses. This afternoon it was a horse. I was over near Bunessan—there's a horse over there that's rather long in the tooth. As is the owner. It's about time both of them retired, but he insists on riding this poor creature, even though he—the horse—is going on for fourteen. And he—the owner, that is—has put on a lot of weight."

Stuart grinned. "I know who you're talking about. Wallace Spence. Large man. Likes his pies, they say."

"Is that the problem?" said Jill. "He seems to be more rotund every time I see him. And that poor horse of his is buckling under the strain. He reported it lame this afternoon, which is what took me over there. Poor creature. It was obvious to me that he's past carrying Wal-lace about. A ligament gave way—and I don't blame it. I administered a hefty dose of anti-inflammatory, but I think my time would have been better spent in persuading Wallace to give the poor thing a rest."

"Tell him," urged Stuart. "Wallace Spence thinks he knows everything. He doesn't. Tell him to back off and let that poor horse have a well-earned retirement."

Jill smiled. "One shouldn't throw one's weight about too much," she said. "If I told everybody what I thought . . ." She made a helpless gesture. "Where would it stop? There are people who should be told to get rid of their dogs—no argument about it."

Stuart looked at her. "Because there's no point to them?"

Jill shook her head. "I suppose every animal has a point," she said.

"Unlike every one of us," muttered Maureen. "What do they say about some people? A waste of space?"

Maddy laughed. "They say that, don't they? But I've always thought that a bit extreme. You can't call people a waste of space. It's ﹁"

"It's inhuman," said Stuart. "I agree with you, Maddy. Nobody's a waste of space."

"I didn't say they were," Maureen protested, and added, mischievously, "Even if sometimes it seems like it."

Jill persisted. "It's never the animal's fault. It's just that some animals are unsuitable pets. Pythons and so on. People shouldn't keep that sort of thing."

"Tigers?" asked Stuart.

Jill shook her head. "Definitely not. And a tiger would eat you out of house and home."

"And then probably eat *you*," suggested Maddy.

Jill said that was possible. She had read in a veterinary journal of a case in Brazil in which a pet anaconda ate its owner's neighbour. The owner claimed to be uncertain about exactly what happened. He saw that the snake had a large, suspicious lump after the neighbour went missing, but he was unwilling to investigate. A vet was called in by the police, and the snake underwent an operation. The neighbour was found in its stomach.

"Dogs too?" asked Stuart. "Pit bull terriers and so on."

"I don't think they should be kept in the house," said Jill.

"Nor do I," agreed Maureen. "They're a macho accessory—for men. When did you last see a woman keeping one of those creatures? It's always a particular sort of male. Muscle car; muscle dog."

At the end of the dinner, as they were getting ready to leave and people were disentangling coats, Neil said to Jill, "Would you like to come for a meal at my place?"

She did not hesitate. "Of course. I'd love to."

He felt a surge of excitement. "Should I call you?"

She gave him a card with her number on it. "That'll get me."

He felt his heart beating within him. That did not happen every time he met somebody who attracted him: this, he decided, was an entirely different physiological process. He thought: it's happening. And he thought that again, as he made his way back down the track to his house. *It's happening*. Circe. That was nonsense, of course. Stuart should not have mentioned Circe.

He glanced at her. How could anybody ever be in any doubt when they were falling in love? You knew it with utter certainty. You ached. It was an ache, and it could not be confused with anything else. You longed for the other person. You yearned for him or for her. It was an absolute, all-consuming feeling, satisfied only by the presence of the other person, which would confer benediction, give confirmation. And it was no use trying to ignore it, because it was a process of haunting, a taking-over for which there was neither inoculation nor anodyne.

As they left the house, Jill said, "Who's going to the ceilidh next Friday?"

Maddy, who had seen them out into the yard and who was looking up at the stars, turned and said, "Everybody, I imagine." And to Neil, "You must come with us, Neil. It's at the Western Isles Hotel. There's a ceilidh band from Fort William. They're good."

"They're brilliant," agreed Jill.

"Neil?" asked Stuart.

"Yes, I'd love to come."

He caught Jill's eye. She smiled at him. "You'll enjoy it."

He returned her smile. "I'm not all that good at reels and so on. Eightsome reels are all right, I suppose. Dashing White Sergeant, maybe."

"That's enough," said Stuart. "They have a good dance caller. They'll keep you right."

They said good night. Neil walked down the track to his house. It was almost eleven at night, but there was still some light in the sky to the west. The coconut smell of gorse flowers was on the air, and behind it, the smell of the sea. Neil stopped in his tracks and looked up at the sky, still pale blue, even at this hour of night. The moon hung over the hills, a pale disc of white, serene, unconcerned, far enough from the earth as to be indifferent to the human turmoil below. He remembered a line from Seán O'Casey's *Juno and the Paycock*. Joxer Daley, the ne'er-do-well companion of Captain Boyle, gazes heavenwards from time to time and asks of his friend, "What is the moon, Captain? That's the question."

The line occurred throughout the play—Joxer's refrain. It was nonsensical—one of those apparently philosophical questions that meant nothing. The moon just *was*. We just *were*. To search for a meaning beyond that simple fact was pointless.

He looked at the moon.

"What is the moon, Captain?" he muttered.

He stopped. He looked up again. The moon was still unobscured, almost full, floating. He thought: the moon is love, just love, just that. Its distant gravitational pull could not be measured, but it was there, drawing us to people and places we loved. Love was the unseen force that physicists would never explain, because it did not exist in their model of the universe. But we felt it, and it shaped our lives, made us feel elated, or miserable, depending on its charge.

T h i r t e e n

He showed James the bucket in which he had put his share of the catch—six mackerel, glistening silver and green.

"Stuart knows where to find them," said James. "He reads the sea. He sees where the birds are. He watches."

Neil looked down at the fish. He had tried to remember how long ago it was that he had last gone fishing—he would have been fifteen or sixteen, and he had gone fishing with his uncle on a reservoir in the Borders. His uncle had assured him that fish did not feel anything, and yet he had insisted on despatching them quickly, with the small wooden club that fishermen called a *priest*. Neil had not said anything, because he had been determined to appear manly, and men had no compunction in catching fish.

He had accepted Stuart's invitation without thinking about it, and had not been ready for the sudden, wriggling response that came so quickly after he had let the line of feathers drop into the water.

"They're there," said Stuart. "Haul them in."

And up through the waters came the flashes of silver—three mackerel darting from side to side, eventually bursting up through the surface under the tautness of the line. He had worked them off the hooks, their striped flanks slipping through his fingers, shedding scales as he struggled to hold them.

"Nice," said Stuart. "We'll take six each. No need for more just now."

He looked down at the fish as they gasped at the bottom of the bucket. He had killed these silver beings, or was in the process of killing them. He reached down, half intending to retrieve them and throw them back into the sea, but saw that Stuart was watching him. He turned away, leaving the fish to their death. It was like drowning for them, he suddenly remembered. Somebody had once said to him that what fish felt was what we felt when we drowned: the same struggle, the same terror.

Now they were standing outside the house, and he was showing the fish to James.

"I'll cook them," said James. "I'll do them this evening. There's nothing nicer than mackerel that have just been caught. They're every bit as good as sea trout, in my view."

"But you've just arrived," said Neil.

"I want to," said James. "I'm in the mood to cook."

Stuart smiled at James. "When did you get in?" he asked. "I'm sorry I wasn't in for your arrival."

James explained that he had been there for less than an hour. He had called in to say hello to Maddy before making his way down the track. He looked at Neil. "She said you were completely settled in—that you had more or less gone native."

Neil laughed. "Hardly." He thought: I've slowed down; I've been eating my breakfast in my pyjamas; I didn't bother to put on my wristwatch yesterday. Perhaps I have gone native, after all.

Stuart moved away. "We'll see you later. Come up for a drink this evening. Or a meal, if you like."

James gestured towards the bucket of mackerel. "Dinner's planned."

They went inside. In the kitchen, James sat down at the kitchen table. "I've been worried," he said.

Neil lined the fish up beside the sink. "I'm going to have to clean these. I think I remember how to do it."

"A clean incision from the abdomen to the sternum," said James. "Then eviscerate."

As Neil worked, James watched him from the table.

"You said you'd been worried," said Neil. "About what?"

James did not reply immediately, but then, after a few moments, he said, "About you."

"Why me?"

James looked impatient. "Because of your situation. Because of the fact that you're discredited. Because of the fact that it's only because you resigned that you weren't actually dismissed."

Neil waved a hand. "I'm getting over that."

James looked at him with incredulity. "What does that mean?" he challenged.

"Just that," said Neil. "It's unimportant." He paused, and then added, "Now. It all looks a bit different here, if you see what I mean."

James did not. "I don't see what difference it makes—your being on Mull."

Neil tried to explain. "What happened there seems less important here. There are other things to think about."

James shook his head. "It's still important to me."

It seemed to Neil that James was going to say something more, but he stayed silent.

"We can talk about it later, James. I'm going to prepare the fish."

James nodded, and went upstairs. Neil used the tip of the fish knife to penetrate the skin of the mackerel, now stiff in his hands. A line of blood appeared on the fish skin—dark red against the white. The regret he had felt earlier on returned: he had taken this complex creature, with its delicate, pale green stripes, from its natural element. He turned away, feeling slightly sickened.

The mackerel cooked quickly, and was served with new potatoes with butter and a mustard sauce. They talked about the island and about what he had been doing since his arrival. Neil mentioned Jill, and the dinner they had shared at the farmhouse.

"You're interested in her?" James asked, toying with the last of his mackerel.

"I suppose I am," Neil replied. "I like her. She's . . . intriguing."

James raised an eyebrow. "Intriguing? Is that the same as mysterious?"

"No. Interesting. You know how there are some people who are obvious. They don't surprise you when you get to know them better. She's not like that. I feel I don't really know much about her yet, even though I've met her twice, including for a whole evening at Maddy and Stuart's."

James looked thoughtful. "Don't rush."

"You mean: be careful?"

He nodded. "You have to be careful about people you meet on the rebound. You've finished with somebody and you take up with the next person you meet because you're feeling lonely, or rejected, or possibly even a bit unsure as to whether anybody will ever like you again."

Neil lowered his eyes. "I don't feel like that."

"You *think* you don't feel like that," said James.

Neil found himself resenting the intrusion. "I should know how I feel," he said. He tried to hide his feelings, but James picked up the note of irritation.

"Sorry, I don't want to interfere."

Neil said that he had no need to apologise. "I've got over Chrissie," he said. "That's in the past. And I'm not rushing round to find anybody to replace her, although——"

"Yes?"

"Although, as I said to you, I like what I've seen of Jill."

Neil watched James as he spoke. He had been puzzled earlier on as to why James should have been so angered by the Henrietta affair. He had entertained a passing thought that James could be too emotionally invested in him, and that, he thought, was potentially awkward. James was a friend and, as had been made apparent in the events of the last few weeks, he was a good and loyal friend. But it was just friendship, and nothing more—at least from Neil's point of view, and their relationship had not crossed that vague but crucial boundary that separated the platonic from the non-platonic. How those two distinctly different states were distinguished from one another could be a difficult matter. Love was too broad a word to be the basis of the distinction. We loved people with whom we were not *in love*. We loved our friends, but did not love them in the way in which we loved our . . . lovers. That was the key to it, perhaps: *lover* was the term we used for those for whom we had a particular form of affection, usually, but not always, reflected in a physical relationship. You could be a lover in an emotional sense well short of the moment when a relationship became physical.

He looked up at the ceiling. "I'll see," he said. "I promise you— I'm not in a hurry and I won't do anything stupid. I'll see how I feel—and how she feels. I've only just met her."

James seemed to be relieved. "Yes, of course"

"And for the moment, I think I'd prefer not to talk about it, if you don't mind."

James looked hurt. "I just wanted to know. I worry about you. I've told you that."

Neil made an effort. "I understand that, and I'm grateful."

"It's all that horrid woman's fault. It's all down to Henrietta."

Neil shrugged. "I don't really think about her. Especially not here."

James got up from the table. He collected the plates and scraped the mackerel bones into the bin. "I couldn't be like you," he said. "I wouldn't let somebody like that destroy my reputation."

Neil sighed. "My reputation hasn't been destroyed," he pointed out.

"How do you know?"

"Because I don't think anybody has been talking about it. It's a small thing. Nobody particularly cares, I would have thought."

James busied himself with making tea. "This ceilidh," he said. "You'll like it. An island ceilidh is always a good event."

"So everybody says."

They drank tea without saying very much. Neil looked at his watch and announced that he was going to turn in. James said that he would stay up. He had downloaded a documentary that he wanted to watch. "It's about the Indian rail network," he said. "Did you know that I'm wild about trains? I don't tell most people, but I am."

"You could come out as a trainspotter," said Neil—and immediately regretted the remark. But James had not taken offence.

"It's not easy," he said.

Over the next two days, James was kept busy with the painting of the living room and the bathroom. Neil offered to help, but James said it was easier for one person to do it. Neil could make him coffee from time to time and go into Tobermory for supplies. They needed just about everything, he said, apart from mackerel and mussels, which they could get from the sea and the rocks.

Neil met Maddy in town, staggering to their ancient Land Rover under the weight of three stuffed carrier bags. He helped her to load them and accepted her offer of a cup of coffee in the chocolate shop near the pier. She asked him about James, and he explained that he had started the painting of the living room. "It hasn't been done for years," he said. "He's having to clean everything and sand down all the woodwork."

Maddy sighed. "I should do the same. I last painted the kitchen about ten years ago. I've been putting it off."

Their coffee arrived, and she sipped at the layer of foamed milk. "And how is James?" she asked.

He felt that there was something unsaid in this question—as if things had not been going well for James. He replied that he was fine—adding, "As far as I know."

She gave him a searching look. "Do you think he's happy?"

Neil thought for a few moments. "Probably not. Or, shall I put it this way: he's probably no unhappier than most people these days."

This piqued her interest. "You think that, do you? You think that most people are unhappy?"

"To an extent. I don't think that unhappiness is a universal state, if that's what you mean. But I think that it's difficult to cultivate happiness in the face of what's going on in the world."

She took another sip of her coffee. "And what's that? I mean, what's going on in the world?"

He took a moment to answer. Then he said, "Conflict. People adopting an attitude of hostility towards others."

She nodded. "The creation of otherness. Yes, that's exactly what's going on. We live in a time of otherness."

He waited. She said, "Your coffee's going to get cold. That won't help the state of the world, will it?"

They both laughed.

"At least we can get small things right," she said. "We can start by making sure that our coffee is warm, rather than cold. We can do little things that just make it a bit easier for other people. Small acts of kindness, I suppose. Those are easy enough."

He picked up his coffee cup.

"I think that James feels these things more than many others," she continued. "I can tell."

"Because he's gay?" he asked. "Is that what you're saying?"

"Probably. But not necessarily. You can be sensitive and straight, can't you? Gay people don't have a monopoly on sensitivity." She paused. "James understands. It's as simple as that. And it may have nothing to do with his sexuality."

There was a further pause before she continued, "I've always felt a certain wistfulness about him, you know. It's as if he would like things to be otherwise."

Neil thought that she should get to the point. "You're saying that he doesn't want to be what he is? Is that it?"

She looked away, as if embarrassed by a subject that she herself had raised. "James suffers from disappointment. Some people do, you know. They're disappointed in love. They've fallen in love with somebody who isn't available or who can't reciprocate for whatever reason."

Neil was non-committal. "I see."

Maddy warmed to her subject. "It must be terrible. We have one go at life, don't we? One time round, so to speak. And what if you discover that you're not going to be able to get what you really want in this life? What if you're destined to remain in a job that you hate, living in the wrong place, with the wrong person? And you look over the fence, or whatever, and you see there the life that you so desperately want to lead. What then?"

"You're disappointed," said Neil. "Understandably."

"Of course you are. And you feel time slipping through your fingers. And you just want to weep, I imagine." She stared at her cup, now drained of its contents. "That's what I think when I look at those pictures of boats filled with people, trying to get ashore in Europe. What do most of us see when we open the paper and see that? We see a guddle of humanity, heads, limbs, crammed together, on overloaded boats—a mass of others. Not people with names and families and individual stories—just packed humanity. And we daren't think about what's going on in those heads, in those hearts— the longing for something better than the hopelessness they've left behind."

Neil winced. "It's very painful."

"Yes," said Maddy. "It is. And I suppose that most of us know that it's not possible for us to take everybody who wants to come here, because everything would collapse if we did that. We can't house everybody; we can't provide everybody with medical care and a job and a place in a school. We just don't have the space or the resources. And yet our heart says to us that they're people just like us, and if we were in their shoes, we'd do exactly what they're doing—which is to move heaven and earth to get in. We'd do anything—or I certainly would—if the only way I could get a good life for my children was to pile onto a half-sinking boat and make a dash for it."

Neil said, "I understand. I'd do the same, I think." Then he added, "And yet—"

"Yes," said Maddy. "There's a big *and yet*, isn't there? Because when all is said and done, the world is full of unfairness. Those who have won't share with those who haven't, because if they do, they know that the things they value will be taken from them. We're not poor in this country. But if too many others came, then we might be—or at least we'd have far less than we have at present. And nobody—or very few of us—is prepared to give anything up."

Neil saw that she was right. Yet the conclusion depressed him. "So we have to ignore the suffering of others?"

"Nobody wants to," said Maddy, "but in practice people do exactly that. We say that there's a limit to charity."

"You can't give everything away," said Neil. "So there are limits to what can be done?"

"I'm afraid so. We like to think we might create a just society, but I don't see us ever getting there. I wish it were otherwise, but . . ." She looked at him, challengingly. "Name one society in which there's that sort of fairness."

"Sweden?" said Neil, but without conviction.

"Sweden is acutely divided," retorted Maddy. "I have a Swedish friend, Inge, who writes to me. She says that Sweden is two societies now—an unabsorbed society of more recent arrivals and the rest. They're very far apart."

Neil tried to think of another example. "Australia? It's a very egalitarian place, isn't it?"

"If you're there," said Maddy. "But try to get in. The drawbridge is up. Just as it is elsewhere."

"Well, we have to do our best," Neil said. "We have to muddle through, being as generous and as open as we can be, but always realising that we're not going to meet all the demands made of us."

Maddy agreed. " 'Dover Beach,' " she said suddenly. "Matthew Arnold's poem: remember, we talked about it."

Neil remembered. "You said—"

"I said we could talk about it some other time. It haunts me, that poem. That and one or two poems by MacDiarmid—his 'Island Funeral,' for instance. They never go away."

He looked at her. This was somebody who made goat's cheese, and yet allowed herself to be haunted by poetry. And why not? Art was for everybody, not just for the intellectuals in the cafés—if that was where they were to be found.

"Would you mind?" Maddy asked.

"Mind what?"

"Would you mind if I quoted it to you?"

Neil assured her he would not. He glanced towards a neighbouring table, where a middle-aged couple sat, staring out of the window, not talking to one another. *They've said everything they have to say to one another,* Neil thought. Years of silence lay ahead of them.

But then he heard the man say, "There's nothing to do." He spoke in the accent of somewhere far to the south—Liverpool, perhaps.

"I told you. There's nothing to do in Scotland."

He looked disgruntled. "I was the one who wanted to stay at home."

"Too late," she said.

Neil suppressed a smile. He glanced at Maddy, who arched an eyebrow.

" 'Dover Beach,' " Neil reminded her.

"Yes." She lowered her voice:

"The sea is calm tonight.
The tide is full, the moon lies fair
Upon the straits: on the French coast the light
Gleams and is gone; the cliffs of England stand,
Glimmering and vast, out in the tranquil bay.
Come to the window, sweet is the night air!
Only, from the long line of spray
Where the sea meets the moon-blanched land,
Listen! You hear the grating roar
Of pebbles which the waves draw back, and fling,
At their return . . ."

She paused. He was silent. The poetry hung in the air between them. Then he said, "It's very beautiful, isn't it?"

"It is," she said. "And it continues in that vein:

Sophocles long ago
Heard it on the Aegean, and it brought
Into his mind the turbid ebb and flow
Of human misery . . ."

He caught his breath.

"Yes," she said. "Human misery. Listen to this:

The Sea of Faith
Was once, too, at the full, and round earth's shore
Lay like the folds of a bright girdle furled.
But now I only hear
Its melancholy, long, withdrawing roar,
Retreating, to the breath
Of the night-wind, down the vast edges drear
And naked shingles of the world."

He said, "How do you remember so much? I'd like to remember poetry, but it doesn't seem to stick."

"I remember it because I love it so much," she said. "I sit in my kitchen and I read these things and I practise them. Grouse listens to me from his bed—he loves 'Dover Beach.' It means something to him. I know that sounds ridiculous. He wags his tail—which is quite active, by his standards."

"Very," said Neil, smiling.

"The Victorians used to read Homer to babies in the womb," Maddy said. "We don't do that, but we play Mozart to them. Apparently, they can pick it up through the mother's abdomen. They hear the beat."

"Why do you like it so much?" asked Neil.

"Because it says so much about our own time. We live in a very similar moment to Arnold's. He was talking about the retreat of religious faith and the sense of emptiness that people felt when that happened. We should probably talk about values rather than religion. We're witnessing the defeat of values—of virtues, perhaps. That's the tide that's going out."

"Yes," said Neil.

"*And ignorant armies clash by night* . . . That's another line. Don't we see that? Don't we see that all the time? In the rioting streets, in the trenches of the battlefields along the fringes of the few surviving empires. The ignorant armies patrol and clash, and hurl petrol bombs and rockets, and young men die just as they died in Matthew Arnold's day."

"Yes." Neil's voice was small.

Fourteen

The band could be heard from outside. Stuart had parked on the road below, near the lifeboat station, and as they made their way on foot up the steep approach to the bulky Victorian building that was the Western Isles Hotel, they heard the familiar strains of "Mhairi's Wedding" drifting down from above. Beneath them lay the bay, with its lining of brightly coloured buildings and its boats, moored and at anchor. Neil turned round and looked out over the narrow sound that at that point separated the island from the mainland. It was just after nine, and the evening sun was still on the hills of Morvern on the other side. At that time in summer, darkness would not come until well after ten, and even then would be half-hearted, as if the sun could scarcely be bothered setting before it was due to appear again with the early dawn.

The band had settled in beside the bar in a long morning room, now cleared for dancing. There were four musicians: two fiddlers, an accordionist, and a drummer. The drummer was a wizened figure wearing pebble-thick glasses, who glanced from time to time at a music stand loaded with printed music and, seemingly inspired by what he saw, redoubled his efforts. The accordionist, a tall woman with her hair tied back in a ponytail, smiled encouragingly at the fiddlers, who were both much younger.

"That's Lizzie," Maddy said as they went into the room. "She's going places."

The accordionist spotted Maddy, and smiled in her direction.

"The drummer is her Uncle Jimmy," Maddy said. "He takes a drink, as they say in these parts."

Stuart leaned over to whisper to Neil. "More than one drink," he said. "You know the evening's over when Jimmy falls off his stool. Not before."

A number of people had already arrived, and soon there were more, congregating around the bar and spilling over into the next-door room, where more chairs had been set out. They found a place to sit while James ordered drinks. Several people nodded to Stuart and Maddy and one came over to greet them. "Everybody's here," said Maddy, looking about her. "It's the band. People know how good they are."

James brought the drinks back on a tray. He said to Neil, "These people know who you are. They said at the bar: 'So, that's your doctor friend.' They know, you see. Everybody knows what's going on."

Stuart smiled. "No anonymity here, I'm afraid."

"Who wants anonymity?" asked Maddy, taking a sip of the glass of wine that James had bought her.

James glanced at Neil. "Probably nobody."

The band had reached the end of "Mhairi's Wedding."

"That's Mhairi out of the way," said James. "Married off after one hundred and twenty bars of music, plus repeats."

"Do you think she was happy?" asked Maddy.

Stuart looked puzzled. "What an odd question."

James smiled. "If she wasn't, it would have been a lament. Some-

thing like 'Lochaber no More.' Mhairi was happy with her man—
no doubt about it."

The accordionist stepped forward and announced the first dance,
an eightsome reel. Maddy put down her drink. She said to Neil,
"You don't have to, if you don't want to. Dancing's not compulsory
here."

The sets took to the floor, and the band began the fast-paced
music that would get the reel going. Neil watched, as did James,
as the dancers moved round in circles. Several of the men were in
kilts, and several of the women had tartan shawls draped across
their shoulders. There was colour and pace and the occasional
whoop from the dancers. The accordionist grinned as she worked
her magic.

Neil looked around. Jill had said that she would be there, but he
could not yet see her. People were still arriving, though, and before
the eightsome reel was finished, he had spotted her, standing at the
other end of the room, watching the dancers. He saw that she was
with a small knot of people. He noticed the man next to her, who
was wearing a dark green kilt and a blue jersey. She was talking to
him in an animated way, and Neil saw that she was touching his
forearm, as if to emphasise a point. The man listened and nodded,
then bent forward to whisper something to her. Her face broke out
into a broad smile.

James followed Neil's gaze. "Your friend Jill," he said, pointing
across the room.

Neil nodded. "Yes. I can see her." He could see that James had
observed the same thing that he had. He pretended indifference; he
did not want James to see how he felt. He'd had enough of other
people speculating as to his emotions, and so he said nothing more,
and looked away.

James was watching Jill. Now he said, "He's a wildlife

photographer—that guy with Jill. He's Dutch. He's called Dirk. He lives down near Spelve."

Neil nodded.

"He makes documentaries too. For the BBC—and others. He made a film about basking sharks off Coll."

Neil allowed himself another quick glance in Jill's direction. The man had his arm around her shoulder. He looked away quickly, but James had once again noticed. He gave Neil a searching look. "It looks as if—" he began.

Neil cut him short. "Yes, I can see."

James winced. "Sorry."

Neil regretted his curtness. James was his old friend. He was enjoying his hospitality. There was no real reason for him to be short with him. Now he tried to explain. "All right, I was hoping . . . But it's not the end of the world, is it?"

"No," agreed James. "It isn't. Not really. And anyway, you've only just met her."

"I know. I know."

"But it can still feel raw, can't it?"

Neil turned to James. "Why do we make life complicated for ourselves?"

"Simple," replied James. "Biology. Hormones."

Neil grinned. "I'm in my thirties. I thought hormones were a teenage thing."

"You should know better," James retorted. "Or, rather, *we* should know better. We both did endocrinology at the same time. Professor Stevenson—remember him?"

Neil remembered the spare figure of the professor of endocrinology. "He told me I was going to fail. I took him seriously, until I found out he said that to everybody. It was his way of encouraging students. Very thoughtful."

They were interrupted by the sound of somebody tapping on

a microphone. A man with unkempt hair was standing beside the accordionist, holding a microphone from which a black cable dangled. "For all the fishermen among you," he began.

This brought throaty cheers from a huddle of men around the bar.

" 'The Shoals of Herring,' " said the man.

"Aye," shouted a man from the bar. "You sing that, pal."

The man looked at the accordionist, who nodded, and played an opening chord.

"I love this song," said James. "I always have."

The singer began his story of being on a fishing lugger following the shoals of herring.

After the final verse, there was a short silence, followed by applause. The singer handed the microphone back to the accordionist, and bowed.

"Aye, Alistair," called out one of the men at the bar. "Aye."

Alistair grinned.

"That was Alistair," the accordionist said into the microphone. "And now we'll have a 'Dashing White Sergeant' if you ladies and gentlemen will rise to the occasion." She looked across the floor. "You too, Helen. And you, Kenny. Nae sitting around and letting all the other folk do the work."

Neil saw Jill walk onto the floor with Dirk. He was teasing her about something, and she was laughing in response. Neil thought: Why did she agree to meet me for dinner when she was clearly involved with this man? He did not think that she had seen him yet, and he half turned, so that his back would be to her should she look in his direction.

"Are you uncomfortable?" asked James.

"No," said Neil. "I'm not uncomfortable."

"We could go somewhere else," James suggested. "We could go down to the Mishnish and have a drink down there."

Maddy overheard this. She had been talking to a friend at a neighbouring table; now she looked at Neil and James with some concern. "Are you two not enjoying yourselves?"

Neil said that they were. It was not strictly true: James might be, but since he had seen Jill with her Dutch friend, the evening had taken a rather different turn for him.

" 'Shoals of Herring' is a favourite of mine," said James. "I imagine that young man—a boy, really, having to work on deck alongside the others—and wanting to be a man like the rest of them. He says, 'Take your turn on watch like the other fellows.' That makes me feel so sad—I don't know why, but it just does."

Maddy said, "There's something poignant about aspiration—about wanting to be something when you're not—or not yet."

Stuart had drifted off to the bar; now he came back and said something to Maddy that Neil did not catch. The two of them conferred, and then Stuart said to Neil, "I'm going down to the harbour with a friend back there. Rob." He nodded in the direction of the bar. "He's a deputy to the harbourmaster when he's away. And he's away now, apparently. And something's cropped up. He's just had a call." He paused. "Do you want to come?"

James accepted quickly. "Why not?" And to Neil he said, "Come on. You can come back here afterwards."

Neil looked across the floor to where Jill and Dirk were now sitting together, deep in conversation. He had looked forward to the ceilidh; now he wanted to get away. This was his opportunity for doing so without appearing to be rude to Stuart and Maddy, whose guest he was. He asked Stuart what it was.

"A boat has put in," came the reply. "The crew has fled. The skipper seems a bit confused—as if he's concussed, Rob says. He was going on about crew problems, but now he's run away as well—or so it appears. Nobody knows what's going on. Rob has to go down and check up on it. The police are coming to take a look tomorrow, but until then it's all up to Rob."

Maddy declined. "I'm not going off to look at boats. I'm staying here."

They went to the bar. Rob, a tall, powerfully built man in a blue fisherman's jersey, greeted them and then downed the last of his beer. "You're all coming to take a look?" he said. "That's fine. A Russian boat. A bit of a *Marie Celeste*. No crew, and now no skipper. She's tied up on the pontoons, but she can't stay there forever."

"Odd," said Stuart.

"Very," said Rob, reaching for his coat from a bar stool.

The boat was considerably bigger than those around it— at least sixty or seventy feet—a small ship, really, and in dire need of a coat of paint. It was a working vessel, not a fishing trawler or a tug, but clearly too shabby and too functional in its appearance to be a pleasure craft. The hull was light blue while the superstructure, once white, was now a faded beige shade, scratched and discoloured through use and neglect. Too small to be a freighter, its most likely use was as a small inspection vessel of some sort, perhaps one used to ferry crews out to oil rigs. On the stern, the vessel's name and home port, Saint Petersburg, were inscribed in Cyrillic script. A bedraggled Russian merchant marine ensign drooped from a small aft flagstaff.

They stood on the harbour pontoon to which the boat had been secured. Rob shook his head. "The skipper spoke to my assistant when they came in this morning," he said. "He said they wanted to tie up for a day or two, but he didn't make much sense, and his English was poor. There was clearly something going on. There was a lot of shouting. Then everything went quiet until this evening, when we heard that the crew were seen boarding the ferry to Oban. Then the skipper disappeared. Everything's switched off, it seems." He gestured to the gangway that had been lowered from the boat's side. "I think we can take a look."

Stuart looked doubtful. "Are we allowed to go on board?"

"I am," said Rob. "I'm acting harbourmaster and I have the right to board vessels when necessary. You can join me at my invitation."

Neil was uncertain. "I'm not sure," he began. "What if—"

"Come on, Neil," said James.

They followed Rob up the gangway and onto the vessel's narrow deck. There was that strange marine smell, that combination of diesel oil and rope that is characteristic of ships, an acrid mixture that seemed to go with the shabbiness and untidiness of the boat's foredeck. There was a large wheelhouse midships, and the door of this was half-open. Rob went towards it, pushed it fully back, and stepped inside. Stuart and James followed him, while Neil brought up the rear.

At the back of the wheelhouse there was a companionway leading below. It was dark and uninviting. The air in the wheelhouse was stale, and it would be even staler down below. Ships that sailed through rough seas had a particular odour to them, a lingering miasma of seasickness and damp clothing. "Engine room and crew quarters," said Rob, inviting the party to follow him.

Neil felt himself a trespasser. Rob may have had the authority to inspect this vessel, but the rest of them were voyeurs. He gave Stuart a sideways look. "Do you think that—"

Stuart smiled his encouragement. "There's nobody on board," he said.

"Yes, but—"

Rob intervened. "I'm entitled to ask for help in executing my duties," he said. "Law of the sea, or whatever."

"There you are," said Stuart. "Law of the sea. What more do you want?"

James seemed unfazed. "No harm in looking," he said.

Neil followed them reluctantly as Rob led the way down below. He had taken a torch from his pocket, and this was the only illumination in the darkened and silent confines of the boat's lower deck.

The torch beam played across a door that was half-open, shining into a small cabin beyond. Neil saw a couple of bunks and a pile of abandoned clothing on the floor—a dark oilskin jacket, thick socks. Rob moved the beam of the torch up to the wall behind the bunks: photographs cut out and pasted onto the surface—a woman's face, two small children standing hand in hand. It was a small, personal touch that made Neil catch his breath. The occupants of this cabin had vanished, he had been told, but how did one vanish in a time of closed-circuit television and electronic monitoring? Were they being trafficked? People were the most lucrative commodity for any ship to carry, and it was feasible that this might be what had happened here. A boat itself might easily be abandoned by traffickers once the human cargo had been delivered.

He asked Rob, as they moved down the short corridor. "Trafficking?"

"Could be."

The torch was played on another door, closed this time, labelled in Cyrillic script. "Anybody know Russian?" asked Rob.

There was a faint scraping sound. They stood quite still.

"Was that something?" asked Rob.

Stuart answered, "Inside."

Rob hesitated, but only briefly. He stepped forward and knocked loudly on the door. "Harbour authorities," he said.

They listened, but heard nothing. Now Rob reached forward and tried the door handle. It moved, and the door yielded to his pressure. The torch beam lit up the interior of another cabin, at the back of which was a small iron cage. There was a strong smell, and movement; a snuffling, and then a whine.

"Dogs," said Rob.

They stared at the two small bundles of fur. The light of the torch fell on two pairs of animal eyes.

"Poor things," said James. "Poor wee things."

Fifteen

The following day Neil and Stuart drove to the veterinary surgery in the old Land Rover. Jill welcomed them at the door, ushering them into a small, cramped waiting room while she finished a consultation. Neil glanced at the magazines on the table, and thought about how it was a magazine, picked up at random in a Turkish barber's shop in Glasgow, that had resulted in his being where he was now. Waiting room magazines inevitably had a well-used look to them, and these were no exception. A farming magazine, two years out of date, promised an article on cereal prices and a review of tractors; the tattered cover of *Rod & Line* optimistically showed a large salmon leaping on the hook. "Doctored," muttered Stuart. "There are no more salmon like that."

"Fishermen are believers," Neil said. "They have their own sort of faith. It sustains them."

The door on the other side of the waiting room opened and a boy of about twelve emerged. He was carrying a small travel cage in which a battered-looking black cat lay crouched, glaring out at the world through angry, slit eyes. The boy looked at Stuart and smiled.

"Donald," said Stuart. "That's your Sammy, isn't it?"

"Yes," said the boy. "He's been fighting." He spoke with the soft voice of the island. His hair was dark, tousled across his forehead.

Jill appeared behind him. "Again," she said. "Cats never learn. They're far too proud. Sammy seems unwilling to hang up his gloves. His ears suffer as a result, I'm afraid."

Neil saw the ripped ears, one of which had just been sewn up.

"Donald is our neighbour's son," said Stuart.

Jill caught Stuart's eye. An unspoken message passed between them. Neil remembered something being said about the neighbouring farmer. He tried to remember what it was, and after a few seconds it came to him: he did not get on with the vet, or she with him.

Sammy hissed, and Donald bent down to reassure him. He spoke in Gaelic.

"A number of cats on this island only speak Gaelic," Jill said, with a smile. "Sammy's one of them."

"His Gaelic is very good," said the boy. "He much prefers it if I speak to him that way."

"It's a courtesy," said Stuart.

Donald thanked Jill and left. Jill closed the door behind him and turned to Stuart and Neil. She glanced at Neil briefly in a slightly puzzled way, and then addressed Stuart.

"Last night," she said, and then stopped.

"Yes," said Stuart. "A bit of a surprise, I'd say."

She sat down opposite them.

"It was good of you to leave the ceilidh," said Stuart. "I didn't want to disturb you, but it was a bit of an emergency."

She shook her head. "Of course it was. Animal welfare is always an emergency."

"Well, it was just as well you came," said Stuart. "I don't think we would have known what to do."

Neil agreed. Stuart had called Jill from the boat, and she had arrived at the harbour fifteen minutes later—the time it took for her to be driven down and dropped off. She had been taken on board and shown into the cabin where the two puppies were caged. She had crouched down to examine them, muttering something under her breath.

She had been decisive. They should remove the animals immediately, leaving them in their cage, and then somebody should drive her, and the cage, back to her surgery. She would house them there overnight and they could meet the following morning.

"I'll give them a quick check-up," she said. "Dehydration is the most pressing danger. I'll get some fluid into them."

Rob and Stuart had carried the cage up between them, the two small creatures whimpering and gnawing at its bars.

"They're very pretty," Neil said. "Huskies? Do you think they're huskies?"

Jill was non-committal. "Possibly."

"I assume we should tell the police about this," said Rob. "We'll be seeing them tomorrow."

Jill hesitated. "Leave it just now," she said. "I can have a word with them in due course."

Rob frowned. "But animals make it a bit complicated . . ."

She cut him short. "Yes, but I'll handle it." She paused. "It's what I do."

Now, in her waiting room, Jill said, "They were all right overnight. I fed them and they seem to be in good enough condition."

She looked at Stuart. "Did you go back to the ceilidh?"

"Just for a very short time," he replied. "Maddy was ready to leave, and Neil here was—"

"Tired," said Neil.

Jill nodded. "There'll be another." She looked down at her hands. "I need to talk about the dogs."

"Of course," said Stuart. "I suppose you'll need to know what happens about the boat. They obviously belong to the Russians—and they seem to have disappeared. Is there a pound somewhere? Fort William? Oban?"

"There's a place in Fort William," Jill said. "It's attached to the police station. But I'm not too keen on handing animals over to the police. They're not necessarily experts in dealing with waifs and strays—animal ones, that is." She looked intently at Stuart. "And there's an issue here. There's something . . . well, problematic."

Stuart and Neil waited. Jill glanced at Neil. "Where's your friend?"

"James?"

"Yes."

"He's back at the house. He's painting. But what's the complication?"

"These pups aren't exactly huskies."

"No?" asked Stuart. "So what are they?"

"Wolves," said Jill. "Wolf cubs—sort of."

They looked at her in astonishment.

"Actually," Jill went on, "it's hard to tell. But I'm pretty sure that if they aren't purebred—and I don't think they are—then they're a cross between dog and wolf. The two are compatible. You can cross a dog with a wolf, for example, and get something that's in-between. There's not much science to it. Nature will look after it if you put a receptive female wolf in with a male dog."

Stuart drew in his breath. "You mean those two little fellows are hybrids?"

"I think so," said Jill. "There are people in Canada and the US who go in for these cross-breeds. I've not heard of anybody doing it in this country."

"Why not?" asked Neil.

"Because there aren't many wolves. There are some in captivity, of course—but not many. And then you have the Dangerous Wild Animals Act, which requires you to have a licence to own a wolf or anything with a large dose of lupine DNA."

"Can we see them?"

Jill hesitated. "Yes, I suppose so. But you mustn't handle them."

Neil asked if they were dangerous. "They don't look as if they could do any harm."

Jill pursed her lips. "They're wild animals. They may have dog genes in them, but they're wild animals." She seemed to relent. "I can see why you would want to handle them, though. They're very appealing."

As they rose to follow her to the back of the house and into the yard, she said, "I'm only surmising that they're cross-breeds. They don't seem quite right for wolf cubs, judging from photographs I've seen." She paused. "And I suspect these youngsters have been bred in captivity."

"Why?"

"Because in the wild it would be difficult to get wolf cubs from their mother. I wouldn't care to try, at least."

"But I don't get it," said Stuart. "Why would these cubs, or whatever they are, be on a Russian rust bucket in Scottish waters?"

"I have a theory about that," said Jill, as she unlocked the door of a wooden outhouse. "I think they were destined for a purchaser somewhere in Britain—or Ireland, perhaps—for somebody who was tickled by the idea of owning a wolf, or something close enough to a wolf. There are people like that who would be prepared to pay a lot of money for the privilege."

"Strange," said Stuart.

Jill did not agree. "Look at what people spend large sums of money on. Just look. They'll pay immense amounts for the pleasure of knowing that they own something unusual—something that other people haven't got."

They entered the outbuilding and found themselves in a large room lined with animal cages of varying sizes. "This is my overnight stay set-up," said Jill. "It's a sort of recovery ward, I suppose."

Two bundles of fur stirred in the cage nearest the door. Jill went to stand next to the cage. "Here they are," she said. "This one is Harris and this is Lewis. I decided to name them after an island."

Stuart and Neil peered into the half-light; there was a wire descending from the roof, but it had no bulb. They watched as Jill reached into the cage and extracted one of the cubs. As she gave it a pill, it licked at the tips of her fingers and then tried to gnaw them.

"They have sharp teeth," Jill said. "Even at this stage."

Neil saw their yellow eyes and the pert, triangular ears. He said, "What are you going to do?"

Jill put the cub back into the cage and extracted the other. "They're under sentence of death," she said.

Stuart frowned. "Are they ill?"

She shook her head. "If I report them to the animal health people, they'll be taken away immediately. They would be put into quarantine—"

"Rabies?" asked Stuart.

"Yes. But they would be put down pretty soon after that."

"That seems hard," said Stuart. "Couldn't they be rehoused?"

She had already thought of that. "It would be difficult. Who would want an unruly creature? That's what they'll be, you know. Those wolf and dog hybrids aren't easy. I've read about them. It's not like keeping an ordinary dog."

"There must be somebody," said Stuart, and added, "Couldn't you keep them for a while?"

Jill sighed. "That's just putting off the evil day." She lowered her voice. "I'm running a real risk. I should hand them over to the veterinary authorities more or less immediately."

"But that'll be the end of them?" asked Stuart.

She nodded. "Yes."

"So what are you going to do?" asked Neil.

It took her a few moments to reply. She averted her eyes as she replied. "I don't know. I'll see."

She had a farm call to do and had to leave. Stuart and Neil drove off before she did. On the way back, Stuart talked about cubs. "People have been talking about reintroducing wolves into Scotland— just as they've done with beavers."

"They raise rather different issues," said Neil. "Beavers don't kill sheep."

"I suppose they don't," said Stuart. "Yet they were here, you know. There's that story about the last wolf in Scotland being killed back in the first half of the eighteenth century. Before they were hunted to extinction, our forests were said to have been full of them."

"We're incorrigible killers, aren't we?" Neil remarked. "I mean *Homo sapiens* are. We loved killing anything we couldn't husband and eat. Just because they were there. Vast herds of bison. All that big game in East Africa. All slaughtered."

Stuart shook his head. "And there are still people who hunt. You can shoot a lion somewhere, I imagine, if you're prepared to pay enough for it. Elephants too."

"Of course you can. But what's the difference between a pheasant and a partridge?" Neil asked. "Each is . . . what? A life that's important to the creature itself."

A note of anger crept into his voice. "Bigger prey, of course, gives bigger kicks, I suppose. You can stand with your foot on top of your victim. Look what I've killed. Like the king of Spain, not all that long ago. The one who eventually abdicated. He shot an elephant in Botswana and was pictured standing proudly in front of it. The poor creature's lying with its tusks up against a tree—brought to an abrupt end by this man with his rifle. A big life ended by a small, grinning biped."

They drove on in silence. There was pain everywhere, Neil thought. Life was impossible without there being suffering, somewhere, for some being. But why should we add to it? Why should we increase the toll when there is no need? Whatever atavistic urge prompted hunting for pleasure, the fact remained that it was about taking joy in the killing of a fellow creature. Perhaps that lay at the heart of it. Perhaps the death of our animal victim constitutes an assertion of our own life, a triumph over death.

There was a sharp turn in the road, and then a rise up ahead. Once they reached the crest of that, they looked down towards the sea-loch, to Stuart and Maddy's house and James's cottage, and the sea beyond.

"Did you see how she handled that cub?" said Stuart. "Did you notice it?"

Neil was not sure. "Gently?"

"Oh yes, very gently. You could see the love."

Neil said, "She's in the right job, then, isn't she?"

"And yet she's going to have to give them up."

"I assume so," said Neil. "Vets have their rules. It would be unethical for a vet to conceal animals who need to go into quarantine. Or wild animals for which you need a licence. She can't do that."

"No," said Stuart. "Even here."

Neil was intrigued. "Even here?"

Stuart smiled. "You must have picked it up. Things are different on islands. Laws are made in Edinburgh these days, but I'm not sure they get as far as the islands. Not all of them."

They reached the farm. Stuart offered to run Neil down the

track, but he said that he would walk. The day had started cloudily, but now the sun had appeared and there was warmth in the air. The sea was an intense blue, although here and there the wind made the wavelets white.

As Neil reached the house, he saw that James was looking at him through the kitchen window. He waved, and James returned the greeting before coming out to meet him.

"I've some news for you," he said. "Something from Edinburgh."

They went into the kitchen together. Neil noticed that James's jersey was covered in splashes of white paint. "You've been busy."

"Yes, I'm getting there. At least some of the paint is getting to the walls."

"It'll look good," said Neil.

James did not seem interested in discussing the redecoration. "I had a call from Edinburgh," he said. "From Alan."

"Which Alan?"

"The toxicologist. Poisons Alan."

Neil warmed his hands against the range. Even in midsummer, there could be a chill in the air from the Atlantic.

"Henrietta," said James. "We have the means to deal with her. Finally. Completely. We can send her back to Dublin or wherever with her tail between her legs."

James watched the effect of his announcement on Neil. He seemed disappointed when Neil received the news impassively. "Aren't you pleased?" he asked.

Neil shrugged. "You'll have to tell me what it is."

"It's delicious," said James. "It's exactly the sort of thing I like to see. A bully exposed. Somebody getting a taste of her own medicine—with interest."

Neil sat down. He thought that James was looking pleased with himself. "You'd better tell me."

James poured himself a cup of coffee from a coffeepot that had been perched on a warm corner of the range. "Right," he began. "I heard from Alan. He doesn't like Henrietta—who does?"

Neil shrugged. "She has friends. Everybody has."

James made a dismissive gesture. "Not many, I bet. She's the sort who uses people. She'll cultivate you if you're useful to her, but there won't be anything behind it."

Neil looked away. James was showing a vindictive side that he did not like. He wondered whether he should say something—whether he might make some remark about charity, but he decided against it. He did not like to preach.

"Anyway," James continued, "one of the administration people came to see him—Alan, that is. She also doesn't like Henrietta, apparently. There was some issue over the holiday rotation, and she felt she had been treated unfairly. She had been dealing with expenses claims—she puts them in to the Finance department. Conference expenses and so on." He paused. "Henrietta loves her conferences."

Neil nodded. "She does. She's away a lot."

James smiled. "I've heard she gives the same paper wherever she goes."

Neil said he thought that was probably untrue.

"Well, twice then," conceded James. "Let's call it recycling. She has a green agenda. If you write a paper, then make sure you don't deliver it only once."

"Go on," said Neil.

"Alice—that's the admin person—was processing a claim that Henrietta had put in for hotel expenses in London for some infectious diseases conference. Three nights at a hotel somewhere near Regent's Park. Normally that sort of thing goes through on the nod. No difficulty. Not this time."

Neil waited.

"The admin woman happened to have overheard something in the coffee room. It was some weeks after the conference. Henrietta was talking to Chrissie about her trip to London. She was telling her that it was very handy for her—she had a cousin who lived down in London and she had stayed with her during that conference. She said that the cousin's flat was close to Queen Mary's, where the conference was being held." He paused, allowing his revelation to sink in. "You see? Very handy. A chance remark, but pretty significant, I'd say. So she went and looked closely at the hotel receipt that Henrietta had put in and discovered that it was a year out of date. Nobody ever looks at the fine print on these things—they look at the figure at the end. In this case it was eight hundred pounds, or just over."

"But it was from that hotel?" asked Neil.

"Oh, yes. She must have stayed there before—on some other occasion—and used the receipt to claim expenses. This was photocopied. The original one would have been put in the year before, but she kept a copy and used it again."

"Recycling," muttered Neil.

James liked that. "Exactly," he exclaimed. "A good scheme. Don't you think?"

Neil put his head in his hands. "This is awful."

James was watching him. "Awful? Of course, it is. It's awful. She's awful. She's always been awful. But at least now we can do something about her."

Neil asked whether Alan had raised the matter with anybody else. Had he thought of going further up the line, to the director?

"I talked to him about that," said James. "He hasn't done anything yet. He doesn't want to do it himself because there are whistleblower issues. He's employed by the institute. Henrietta has influence. It could rebound on him."

Neil said he could understand that. It was often difficult for whistleblowers, who might be victimised for doing the right thing.

"He thinks the person to do it is you," James continued. "You no longer work there. A former member of staff makes a much more secure whistleblower."

James looked at Neil expectantly.

Neil rose to his feet and went to the window.

"See anything outside?" asked James.

"I'm thinking."

"What's the sea doing?"

Neil felt a momentary irritation. James was crowing. He was enjoying this.

"I need to think."

"Well, have a think," James said. "Then, when you've finished thinking, we can get back to Alan." He got to his feet and came to stand next to Neil and put a hand on his shoulder, Neil moved away slightly, instinctively, but James appeared not to notice, or not to care.

"You have to do it," James said. "It's your civic duty. This is criminal conduct—apart from anything else. We all have a duty to report crime."

"I said that I'd think about it," snapped Neil.

"Good. But there's only one conclusion you can reach, you know. It's the one staring you in the face."

"And that happens to be the one you're suggesting."

James grinned. "Yes. A complete coincidence, but yes."

Sixteen

He tried to stop thinking about it, but it stayed with him all night and into the following morning. He could not rid his mind of the challenges that James had so gleefully planted in it. Did he have to act? Were the affairs of the institute still his concern? Did one have to respond to wrongdoing whenever one became aware of it?

He had an early breakfast, by himself. The door to James's room was closed when Neil got up and was still shut after he had finished his boiled eggs and toast—his habitual breakfast. He ventured out-side to check on the weather. It was dry, and there was only the slightest of breezes from the sea. There was some cloud to the south, down towards Iona, but in the west, over the stretch of sea between Mull and Coll, the sky was clear.

The questions that had haunted the night were still with him and he decided to walk down to the shore to clear his mind. He saw that the tide was about halfway in, and that here and there in the sea-loch circling terns had picked up the movement of fish. Sprats and sand eels would be moving into the shallow waters at the head of the loch, and would be followed by pursuing mackerel. One or two of the seabirds had made their catch and were already on the shore, pecking at the grounded fish, screeching in protest at the attempts of interlopers to deprive them of their bounty. A large black-backed gull glared at him as he approached, raising its beak in challenge.

He kept away from the gulls and headed to the opposite end of the beach. Shell fragments crunched underfoot; tiny crabs, disturbed by his footfall, scurried sideways into the water. He bent down and retrieved a piece of green glass, polished smooth by the action of the sea. It was old enough, he thought, to be a fragment of the large glass floats that fishermen used to use before the age of plastic. Intact floats no longer turned up on the tideline, but pieces did, reminders of an earlier age of larger fishing fleets and plentiful fish. The world was becoming thinner, less rich in ornaments and interest, as we colonised and consumed its every space, its every resource. Abandoned plastic was immortal; it would never be rubbed smooth by the waves; it would never reflect or distort the light as this piece of glass did; it would never be of a particular time and place, as this detritus was.

He slipped the piece of glass into his pocket and continued along the beach. So, Henrietta was dishonest; should he be surprised? He already knew that she did not care much for the truth, but this was a different sort of dishonesty. Many people are prepared to lie when in a tight spot; those who were prepared to embezzle or engage in outright theft were rather fewer in number, but they were there, of course, and some of them, perhaps a large number, would be in positions of responsibility. Academic institutions were meant to be places of principle and probity, but so many of them had become businesses, focused on economic survival, and had become venal as a result, as everything else seemed to be. Of course, even before the commercial ideal was adopted, these institutions could be hotbeds of careerism and empire building, and so perhaps nothing had changed; perhaps the Henriettas of this world had always found academia the perfect ground for their machinations. Nowhere, it seemed, did you get to the top through niceness.

He gazed up at the sky, almost dizzying in its emptiness. He saw that it was being crossed by a flock of geese, swooping in from Coll, an unwavering V-formation, an arrow tip of birds. He heard the beating of their wings, a pulse of life, and the radio traffic of their calls to one another. He watched as they crossed the low hills of that part of Mull before heading for the Morvern peninsula, with its hidden glens and lochs.

He lowered his gaze and saw a movement ahead of him on the beach, at a place where an outcrop of rock came down to the water's edge. It was Donald, the son of the neighbouring farmer; the boy they had met at Jill's surgery, the owner of the pugilistic cat.

The boy looked at him with the open expression of island children. Neil greeted him. "How's poor Sammy?" he asked. "Is his ear better?"

He was answered courteously. "He's very well, thank you. His ear's healing."

"A nasty injury," said Neil. "Cats are always wrecking their ears."

The boy had with him a fishing net at the end of a long pole. Neil gestured towards it. "What are you going to catch?"

Donald pointed to a rocky outcrop further down the sea-loch. "Sometimes, when the mackerel are running, you can catch them in a net right there, off the rocks. They swim really close to the shore—going after sand eels."

Neil smiled. "Sammy could guddle for them, couldn't he? He could scoop them out. That's how bears catch salmon in Canada."

Donald grinned. "He follows me sometimes—down from the farm. But the gulls chase him away. They don't like cats. And once a buzzard went after him. It swooped, but then changed its mind. My dad says that birds of prey are very careful about not getting injured."

"Of course they are," said Neil. "If they're injured, then that's it."

Donald twirled the net, describing a figure of eight in the air. "The other day," he began. "Yesterday, when you and Stuart were down at the vet's place—"

Neil was cautious. "Yes."

"You know what was in the shed?"

Neil said nothing. Could the boy have seen what was there?

Donald squinted up at him. He was polite, but insistent. "It's wolves, isn't it? She's got a couple of wolf cubs, hasn't she?"

Neil tried not to show any reaction. "There are no wolves in Scotland," he said, smiling. "At least not any longer."

Donald stopped twirling the stick. He hesitated before he spoke. Then he said, "My dad says that she shouldn't. He says that you can't keep animals like that without a licence. You have to get a licence—and he says she hasn't got one."

Neil waited for him to continue, but that seemed to be as much as he cared to say.

"Well," said Neil at last. "I'm not at all sure. Did you see them yourself?"

The boy nodded. "I went round the back. I looked in the shed. I had my dad's phone. He lets me have it when we're in Tober-mory. He was in the Co-op while I was at the vet's place. I took a photograph."

"And?" prompted Neil.

"My dad said they were wolves. He said that he would report her to the animal welfare people. He says there's an office in Fort William."

Neil asked whether that had happened.

"No," answered Donald. "He's going to Fort William next week. I think he'll do it then."

Neil looked over his shoulder towards the edge of the water. The tide was rising visibly, inching its way up the beach, moving small clusters of seaweed. "The mackerel will be waiting for you," he said. "And I need to get on."

The boy nodded, and moved off silently towards the rocks. Neil watched him for a moment before turning and making his way back to the house. James may have emerged, and he would offer to make him breakfast. Then he would drive to Tobermory, where he wanted to pick up supplies. They needed milk, being down to their last half-pint, and he would try to get some of the fresh vegetables that the Co-op had promised would be on the shelves by today. Then he would go to speak to Jill, who needed to be warned about what Donald had just told him. He was conscious of the fact that he was involved in something that was really none of his business, but that, it seemed to him, was the way of things on an island; you were drawn in, you became part of the affairs of the island, even if you were, as he was, a bird of passage.

He had gone out that morning with the intention of clarifying how he felt about the news he had received from Edinburgh. He was no nearer making a decision about that, although he was resolved on one thing already: he would not let James dictate to him what he should do. He would make up his own mind, and would do what he felt was right. At the moment, he was more inclined to do nothing. He had come here to disengage from an unpleasant situation—from involvement in a confrontation that he knew he could not win, not in a world in which positions were struck with such unforgiving intensity. He was not sure that he wanted to return to that particular fray, and yet . . . He was not a coward, and he knew that if he failed to respond to the challenge, he might quite reasonably be accused of cowardice. The barricades in this life, somebody had once said to him, are never in quite the place that we'd like them to be. That did not mean, though, that we were excused from defending them.

He approached the house. Through the kitchen window he could see that there was no light on, which meant that James was still asleep. He kept odd hours, Neil had noticed, and unless he was working would sometimes not surface until midday. Neil would leave a note on the table telling him that he had gone into Tobermory and suggesting that he should call him if there was anything he needed from the shops.

He left the house quietly. In the car on the way up to the top of the hill, his mobile phone uttered one of those little pips by which it marked the receipt of a message. He ignored it, and it was not until he parked in the harbour that he saw what had arrived. Now it said: *Chrissie*, and gave the time of the message.

He hesitated. He was tempted to ignore the message, at least until a bit later. The rawness that he felt over what had happened was there, and he was not sure that he wanted to expose it once again. We're sometimes entitled to get away from things we don't like, he said to himself. There was no point in scratching at the scabs that grew over the wounds of the past. There was too much of that; too much focus on the past when the present was crying out for attention. But then he looked at the screen again and brought up the message.

I'm coming to Mull for a few days, she said. *Can I see you?* And then, finally, the single word: *Please*.

He caught his breath. He was aware of the fact that he was at a crossroad, with two very different directions ahead of him. He could ignore her; he could even reply with a curt refusal, or a denunciation. He could write, *You've got a nerve . . .* or something like that. Or he could rise above all that—the conflict and confrontation that he had decided he would avoid by coming here, getting away from the toxic divisions of public and academic life, from the ruins of wounded tolerance and courtesy. He made his choice.

Of course, he wrote. Then, *When?* And finally, *Love, Neil*. He deleted *love*, and inserted *best*. If we could not live in an age of love, then we could at least inhabit a world of best.

He tapped the screen, and the phone obediently registered the departure of the message with what sounded like a polite burp. Were it a chord, the notes would be: sent; gone; too late.

Jill was surprised to see him. She was packing her bag when he arrived, filling it with a series of bottles and syringes.

"I wasn't expecting you," she said, glancing at her watch. "I have a couple of calls over at Lochaline. I was going to catch the ferry."

"I should have phoned," he said. "I could come back."

She looked at her watch again. "Actually, I'd miss the eleven o'clock ferry anyway. I can go a bit later. It's nothing urgent."

She closed her bag and looked at him. She was about to say something, but he spoke first. "The other night—"

She put up a hand. "I was going to apologise."

He frowned. "For what?"

She looked away. "For not speaking very much to you at the ceilidh. I wanted to, but then you disappeared and I realised that you might have . . ." She trailed off.

"Yes?"

"You might have been offended."

He shrugged. "I don't see what I had to be offended about."

"My ignoring you. I didn't mean to—you know how it is at these things."

He inclined his head. "You were busy. I could see that."

She did not respond immediately, but eventually she said, "Dirk, I suppose. He's . . . he's an old friend—as is his wife. I've known her longer than I've known him—since we were eight. She's not been well."

He waited.

"She was in hospital in Glasgow for three weeks. Now she's back, but it's been a slow business. She's had surgery on her back. That was the first time Dirk's been out for weeks. He was looking after her."

Neil said that he was sorry. "I didn't . . . I thought . . ." He broke off. He was not sure what to say.

But she made a gesture to indicate that they had better things to talk about. "You probably want to see the boys back there." She nodded in the direction of the shed.

He shook his head, which puzzled her. "I thought—" she began.

"Oh, I'd like to see them, but there's something I need to tell you first."

He told her of his conversation with Donald. She listened intently, and winced when he came to the part about the matter being reported to Fort William. "When?" she asked.

He said something about next week.

She relaxed, and smiled.

Neil was puzzled. "I don't want to interfere, but I would have thought this is serious. You have a duty, surely, to ensure that quarantine requirements are met. You don't have wriggle room here."

She said that he was right about the duty.

"Well, then, don't you have to report this to somebody? And, in the meantime, keep the cubs from having any contact with other animals?"

"I do. I have to do both."

But she did not look at all dismayed.

"Well, I'm sorry," he said. "It looks to me as if you're in a bit of a fix."

She laughed—which surprised him further. "We're one step ahead of Donald's father. I've made arrangements. They're going on Tuesday."

"But what about a licence?"

"We're on top of that. I've been in touch with the zoo over in Edinburgh. They'll take them and arrange for them to go somewhere. There are people who keep wolves in enclosures—wildlife parks, that sort of thing. They say they know of somewhere that's prepared to take a hybrid. They'll look after the licence—and handle the quarantine. It'll all be done perfectly legally."

He understood now how she had been able to be so relaxed. "You've been busy," he said.

"Yes. I didn't like the thought of their being put down. Vets have to do that sort of thing—obviously. But we never like it."

He asked about the farmer. "Is there a bit of history there?"

"A lot," she said. "I used to be a government vet—before I took on my small animal practice in Glasgow. It was my first year out of veterinary college and I was pretty green. I had to respond to a complaint that somebody had made that Donald's father was neglecting sheep. He had some grazing on a remote headland. The complaint was that he wasn't attending to them. There was nothing to it, but I had to investigate. He was, as they put it here, *sair offended*. He never forgave me."

"Some people like to hold a grudge," said Neil. "Like Tam o' Shanter's wife—*nursing her wrath to keep it warm*."

Her face lit up. "Burns always puts it so well."

They were both silent for a few moments. Then she said, "We could go and take a look at the boys."

She took him out to the shed. As the door opened, the two cubs got unsteadily to their feet. Their eyes caught the light from the open door. They pressed their noses against the constraining bars of their cage. Neil heard their breathing—a sniffling sound that all young creatures seem to make.

"I've forgotten which is Harris and which is Lewis," Jill said. "But I don't think it matters."

"Of course not," said Neil.

She moved forward, brushing against him inadvertently as she did so. He moved forward to get a better look at her charges. They watched him warily.

Jill whispered. "*I'm truly sorry Man's dominion has broken Nature's social union.*"

She turned to Neil. "More Robert Burns," she said.

"I'm sorry too," he said.

Seventeen

James looked at him with undisguised astonishment. He had been painting a storeroom just off the kitchen, and paint dripped down off the brush he was wielding.

"Be careful," said Neil, pointing to the floor.

James balanced the brush on a tin of paint. "Don't worry about that," he said. "It's only paint. What did you just tell me?"

"I told you that Chrissie's coming to Mull. I've just heard."

James shook his head in disbelief. "That's what I thought you said." He paused. "I thought that I was hearing things, but I wasn't."

Neil shrugged. "She wants to see me. I've said yes."

James muttered something under his breath that Neil did not catch. The he went on, "I find that frankly hard to stomach. After the way she's treated you, you're still prepared to see her and . . . and I imagine that she's after something."

Neil said that she had not revealed what was bringing her to Mull. "I didn't ask—and she didn't volunteer any information. She just asked to see me—politely. She said *please*."

James snorted. "Oh, that's great. She's polite now. She says *please* after she's cheated on you with that . . . that interior designer or whatever and then, just to make sure of things, she conspired with your former boss—the boss who fired you . . ."

"I resigned," Neil corrected him.

"Constructive dismissal," snapped James. "Ever heard of that? It's where somebody has no choice but to resign. That's what happened to you, Neil, whether you admit it or not. She conspired with that ghastly Henrietta to take your job. Now she wants to come and make it up to you."

Neil took a deep breath. "You've got no grounds to say that. Neither of us knows why she's coming."

James's response was more of a sneer. "Oh, there are plenty of reasons to come to Mull. Ornithology. Whale watching. Walks in the hills . . . I'm sure that's what she has in mind. It just so happens that you're here at the same time, and so she does what any faithless lover does—she gets in touch to suggest a meeting over tea or an intimate dinner in the Café Fish."

Neil braced himself for an ill-tempered argument. James was going too far.

"I don't feel as hostile towards her as you do, James—I really don't. And I don't think we should fall out over something like this."

James bit his lip. "I'm only trying to protect you."

"From what?"

"From somebody who has treated you appallingly. From somebody who has taken your job. Is that enough to be going on with?"

Neil crossed to the other side of the room and looked out of the window. The sea was silver in the changing light. The next moment it could be blue. Out towards Tiree, a fishing boat ploughed its way across a stretch of water, heading for the cold depths where the cod would be hunted.

"I think you may be motivated by something other than my protection."

Neil spoke almost without thinking. And the moment he finished, he realised that it was the wrong thing to say. James narrowed his eyes. His mouth opened slightly. This was an unexpected view.

"What do you mean by that?"

For a few moments, Neil said nothing.

James pressed him. "Come on, what did you mean?"

"Nothing much. It's just that I thought you were . . . well, interfering in my affairs. Sorry, but that's what I felt. And also . . ." Again, the words were unguarded.

"Also?"

Neil sighed. "I thought you might be just a bit jealous."

James stood quite still. "Jealous of what?"

Neil felt that he had gone too far to extricate himself. "Jealous of me, I suppose. It occurred to me that you seem dead set on keeping me from Chrissie. And I thought—and I may well be wrong on this—but it crossed my mind that you might want my friendship to yourself. I thought that you might be becoming, well, possessive."

James's eyes were upon him. His expression was impassive.

"I don't mean to offend you," Neil continued. "I may be misreading the situation. Sometimes, I admit, I get things completely wrong."

James lowered his voice. He did not move from where he was standing. "Are you implying—"

Neil cut him off. "I'm not implying anything. I think we should just forget about all this. I really don't want a row. In fact, that's the last thing I want. That's why I came here in the first place."

Suddenly, James stepped forward to draw out a chair from under the kitchen table. He sat down heavily. Neil remained standing.

James looked up at Neil. If there had been any anger in his expression, it had now disappeared. "Why don't you come right out and say it?" he challenged.

Neil shifted his weight on his feet. He felt acutely uncomfortable. He had not intended their conversation to go in this direction, and now he regretted his earlier impetuosity.

"There's nothing to be said," he replied. "I was feeling a bit stressed. I spoke out of turn. Sorry."

But James did not accept that. "I think you knew exactly what you said. I think you said what must have been in your mind. You meant it."

Neil shook his head. "I don't think so."

"Well, I do," retorted James. "I think you're implying that I want you. Isn't that what you're saying? And more than that, you're suggesting that I've got it in for Chrissie because she's a rival. Nice theory. All very neat."

Neil tried to defend himself. "Well, even if there had been a bit of that—even if that had crossed my mind, it's clear to me now that it's nowhere near the truth."

"Why did you think it anyway?" asked James. "Have I given you any reason—the remotest reason to think that?"

Neil brought up the conversation that he had shared with James in Edinburgh, when James had talked about his feelings for somebody who could not return them. "You told me about that," he said. "You volunteered the information—you told me quite openly. But you didn't say anything about where, when, or who—which seemed a bit strange to me. And it occurred to me that you could have been talking about me."

"You?" exclaimed James. "Why would you think it was you?"

Neil shrugged. "I can't put my finger on it. I just thought it might be."

"Well, it isn't," said James.

"So I now know. I'm sorry for jumping to the wrong conclusion."

James was still staring at him. "Do you really want to know about it?"

Neil held up his hands. "Listen, James, I don't want to interfere in your private life. I don't need to know about that side of your life."

"But what if I were to tell you? What then?"

Neil said that it was entirely up to him. "I'd listen if you wanted me to."

James sat back in his chair. "I went to a boarding school, you know. My parents lived in Germany, and then in France, also Canada for a couple of years. The company my father worked for moved him around every couple of years, and so they thought it was better for me to go to a boarding school. I went to a place in Perthshire. It was all right, for the most part. I wasn't unhappy, and I wasn't particularly happy. In-between, I suppose. Most people, I suspect, are in-between.

"At weekends we were allowed home, or, if our parents were abroad, we could go with friends to their houses. I had a friend whose uncle lived on a farm about twenty miles away. The farm was a large one—I suppose you might call it an estate—and there was a river running through it, and a forest that for some reason they called the Lost Wood. Nobody knew why: perhaps people had got lost in it a long time ago. My friend—let's call him David—said that there was a local legend that Rob Roy had hidden there for some time and that he used to carry out raids from the shelter it provided. There was definitely a cave there, but David seemed unwilling to go into it, and we just looked at it from a distance.

"I'm not sure if I sign up to that whole romantic Highlander stuff—you know, the Prince in the Heather and the Jacobite songs and so on—but when you're there, following a burn up a mountain, or watching a group of stags on a hillside, it's easy to feel it. And I liked going there for weekends when David invited me. We put the school behind us and did the things that you did on such places— checking up on sheep and cattle, mending fences, and so on. We went stalking with his uncle once or twice. There was an old stalker from Aberfeldy who went with us. He had an ancient telescope covered with leather, and he would take this out and spot deer while we were all lying in the heather. I liked that part of it, but I did not like the end result—the dragging the deer off the hill using the ponies. The blood seemed to attract the clegs—you know, those vicious horseflies—and they really stung if they managed to get you.

"One weekend we went there, and David's uncle and his wife decided to go off to a dinner party in Helensburgh. David told them that we would be all right—there was a venison casserole in the fridge and we could have that for dinner. They were going to stay overnight in Glasgow, and then come back the following day. We would look after the place, he said. We had just turned seventeen then—it was our last year at school.

"That afternoon we had climbed the hill behind the house. It was late May, almost June, and the weather was warm. We reached the top, where there was a cairn. Every rock, David said, had been placed there by him or by his older brother. He said that I could add one to the pile. He and his brother had always wished for something when they placed their rock there—I should do the same, he said. I found a rock and put it on top of the pile. He was standing behind me. He looked at me and asked me what my wish had been. I told him that you shouldn't reveal what you wished for, or it wouldn't work. I said everybody knew that. But he pressed me for an answer, and eventually I said that I had wished that he and I could remain friends forever. If he was surprised by this, he didn't show it. He said, 'But of course, why shouldn't we?' I didn't know how to answer that properly, but I tried. I said, 'Because people go away. They make new friends.' David shrugged and said, 'I don't see why that should happen.'

"It was late afternoon by the time we got back to the house. He was trying to fix up an old quad bike, and spent some time stripping down the engine. I wasn't much help with that, so I left him to it. At the time I was reading a book by a Dutch doctor who had gone to work in Ethiopia. My father had given it to me, because he had met the doctor somewhere or other and he thought I might be interested in it. I was, and it was that book, I think, that convinced me I had to study medicine.

"When I went into the kitchen later on, David was already there. He had found a bottle of German wine—one of those Piesporters that you like when you're seventeen—and he had poured himself a glass. He offered me one. I wasn't used to wine, but I pretended to be. He raised his glass in a toast and I did the same. He said, 'German wine is a bit too thin for me.' I didn't know what he meant, but I agreed. 'Far too thin,' I said.

"We had our meal. The wine went to my head, but only slightly—and I think it was the same for him. His uncle had a collection of old vinyl records and a turntable. He liked Scottish folk music, and David played me tunes from his collection. There was 'My Love's in Germany.' Do you know that one? *My love's in Germany, Send him hame, send him hame* . . . Whenever I hear that now, I think of then. Music's like that, isn't it? It evokes memories of time and place and how we felt when we first heard it.

"We were tired, and we weren't used to wine. We went up to his room. He said, 'I'm not going to forget this day.' I thought of the words of that song. *Send him hame, send him hame.* I said, 'I like being with you.'

"He looked at me, and smiled. For a brief moment I dared to hope, but then I realised his smile was just an ordinary smile—nothing more than that. He said, "You can have my bed—I'll sleep on the cushions." He took these from a couple of chairs, to lay out on the floor. I lay there in the semi-darkness—it was almost summer, and the light never really fades in Scotland then, as we all know. I stared up at the ceiling. I could tell that he was asleep, but I wanted to stay awake as long as possible, that not a second of this be lost.

"When I woke up, it was four in the morning. I looked at David, across the room. I watched his breathing, the slight movement of his eyelids. The face has a way, I've always thought, of showing us that there's a person inside, even in sleep.

"I got up and looked out of the window, at the trees in their stillness, at the sheep in the paddock beyond the byre. I then experienced a feeling that I had never had before: a sense of profound gratitude that I was alive and that I was there, in the company of somebody who was so important to me, who made sense of a world that I had, until that moment, barely understood. It was a most remarkable feeling—one of complete elation. And then I turned back into the room and realised that what I felt was love. That was all there was to it. And I felt dizzy, as if I had taken a deep draught of champagne and it had gone straight to my head. Everything was precious—the world of the room, of that house, of the hills and sky. Everything was just right—exactly where it was, precious for what it was.

"We went back to school, but we had only a month or so left before we left that place behind. On our final day, the pipe band lined up in the quad outside our rooms and played as we made our way to the hall where our parents were waiting, ready to take us away from this strange, enclosed world in which we had spent the last six years. They played 'Mist Covered Mountains,' which always gets me right here, because it's about leaving and being away from what you love.

"Does that make any sense to you? Perhaps not. But the point I want to make to you is that for some of us there is no alternative but to carry within ourselves a glimpse of something that other people may not be able to understand, or may choose to look down upon, but for us it's no different to what others feel when they fall in love. A memory of love. And it can stay with you for years and years— for your whole life, perhaps. Your whole life."

Neil sat quite still. He wanted to reach out to James, to put his arm around his shoulder and console him. But he sensed that consolation was not what James wanted.

"And David?" he asked.

"It was different for him—obviously. He did not feel the way I felt. That was all there was to it."

"Have you seen him since then?" asked Neil.

James hesitated. Then he replied, "Yes, often."

He looked up the road towards Stuart's house, inadvertently, perhaps. Or perhaps not.

Neil knew then.

He arranged to meet Chrissie in Tobermory. She had suggested the chocolate shop, and he was sitting there at one of their tables, when he saw her walk past the window. She stopped, and waved to him through the glass, over the heads of the people who were sitting in the window alcove. He looked up, and their eyes met. He raised a hand in greeting. His stomach lurched. She was wearing a blouse that he had bought her on impulse once, from a stall in Covent Garden when he had been down in London at King's College. He had telephoned her to check on her size, and she had said, "It's very sweet of you, but be careful, just in case . . ." She had left the proviso unfinished, but had been delighted when he had given it to her. "I love this shade of green," she said. "It's perfect." Now she was wearing it, and it must have been a deliberate choice, to remind him.

She moved forward to embrace him. He wanted to avoid her touch, but he could hardly pull back, right there in public, so he allowed her to put her arms about him and to plant a kiss, a light touch of a kiss, on his cheek. Then he turned his head away, and extricated himself. He felt her hold on to him, her hand upon his shoulder, but he persisted, and he was soon free. To anybody watching us, he thought, we are two old friends meeting after a time apart. Or two former lovers, perhaps, if an observer were to notice my awkwardness.

"So."

It was, he thought, just the right thing for her to say.

"So," he replied.

She smiled. If she was finding this difficult, she was not showing it. "So here we are," she went on. "I'm not sure where to begin. What about you?"

"What about me? I'm here in Mull. I'm going to be around for a few weeks, and then . . . well, back to Edinburgh, I suppose, or Glasgow. Or somewhere. It depends on the job."

He noticed that at the mention of a job, she looked away. As well you might, he thought: you have my job.

"You're staying in public health?" she asked.

"It's what I do, I suppose. But I have an open mind. And this place . . ." He looked about him. They were in a chocolate shop that also did coffee, but they were also in Tobermory, on the island of Mull, with the sea of the Hebrides just over the hill, and the islands beyond. That was what he meant by *this place*. "This place has an effect on you."

"Slows you down?"

He considered this. "Yes, but . . . That's too simple. It helps you to look at things from a different perspective."

She nodded encouragement. "We used to come here on holiday," she said. "I don't think I ever told you. We came here for family holidays three or four times when I was ten, twelve, round about then. And we went to Colonsay too. My father preferred Colonsay, although he never spelled it out because my mother liked Mull, and he always did what she wanted. She did most of his thinking, I suspect."

"That can happen in a marriage."

She shifted in her seat. "Are you all right?" she asked.

"In general? Or right now?"

"In general."

He looked out of the window again, and she followed his gaze. A delivery van was reversing into a tight parking space. The sky was crossed by mewing gulls.

"I'm fine," he said.

"Do you think of me? Ever?"

He shrugged. "Sometimes." Then added, "We were together for some time, weren't we—it would be odd if I didn't think of you."

She leaned across the table. "I think of you often." She paused. "I do, you know. Every day, in fact."

For a few moments, neither said anything. He continued to stare out of the window—he found it hard to meet her gaze, which he sensed was upon him. But now he turned round, and saw that she was looking at him with the expression of one who wanted desperately to say something more, but found, perhaps, that the words eluded her.

At last, he said, "Why did you come?"

She replied quickly, apparently without having to think about it. "To see you." And added, "Of course."

He might have seen the face of the person who had let him down, but he saw only the face of the person with whom he had, for a time, shared his life—the person who was *there*.

Now she continued, "I wanted to see if there was any chance of patching things up."

He had not been prepared for this. He had wondered, of course, about the point of her visit. He had thought it possible that she had come to Mull specifically to see him, but he had discounted the possibility. He was wrong.

She reached out to touch him—a brief touch on the forearm. He looked down at her hand.

"Do you think there might be?" she asked. "We're no longer together—Brian and I."

Brian . . . He had never liked that name. He liked it less now.

Curiously, he was not surprised by this news. Her affair with the interior decorator had seemed to him to be so unlikely—so extreme. It had been a sudden madness on her part—prompted, perhaps, by a feeling of being trapped. Sometimes people panicked; they sensed that possibilities were being closed off too freely, that they were involved in a relationship that might be going too far and too fast for them. Unfaithfulness freed one from the claims of constancy: it could show that you did not care; that you could be free if you wanted to be.

Now she said, "I don't want to put you under any pressure. And I wouldn't be surprised if you said no."

He was still looking at her hand. It was still resting on his forearm. He said, "Really?"

"No, I wouldn't. I treated you badly. Very badly. And I'm sorry."

He looked down at the floor. Somebody had dropped a pencil. Instinctively he bent down to pick it up.

"A pencil," he said.

She frowned. "Yes, a pencil. Somebody must have dropped it." Then, as if impatient to get back to the subject under discussion, she continued, "I wanted you to know that I'm sorry. I regret it."

He muttered, "You regret it."

"Yes, I do."

Now he said, "I'm not sure whether that changes anything."

He could see that she was relieved, in spite of what he had just said. "No, of course not. I'm not asking you to decide right now. You could let time do its thing."

He ignored what she had just said. "I could stay with James for a week or two—maybe a bit more. There's room in his flat, but I don't want to outstay my welcome."

She considered this. "James likes having you to stay."

He was not sure whether this was a statement or a question.

"He does," he said. "Or, at least, he doesn't seem to mind. We lead separate lives."

"I know that. Does he . . ." She hesitated. "Does he have anyone?"

Neil shook his head. "That depends on what you mean by that. The answer is no, in the sense of having a partner. But people have other people in their lives even if those other people are in the past. Not everybody is lucky enough to find somebody . . . well, somebody in the present."

She looked puzzled. "I'm not sure if I see what you mean."

"No matter," he said.

She reached out to touch him again. "I want you to come back," she said. "I want that with all my heart. Does that sound too much? Too dramatic? It probably does. But I'll say it again: with all my heart."

James had been direct.

"You're out of your mind, Neil," he said when Neil came back from Tobermory. "Even seeing her is plain stupid."

"She regrets what happened. She was very clear about that."

James rolled his eyes. "Oh, sure. Sorry, sorry, sorry . . . Enough sorries? That's fine. Nothing happened. All forgotten. Back to how things were before . . . before I cheated on you in your own bedroom—yes, your own bedroom—and became all pally with the woman who effectively had you fired. And then I took a job paid for by the money that had funded your original post. Before all that— which I really regret, by the way. But that's in the past—a couple of weeks ago, in fact. Ages. A lot can happen in that time. A lot. It's time enough for my new friend Brian to go off and rearrange somebody else's life, which means that I need to look around for somebody once more, and so I come to Mull—"

Neil stopped him. "You're cross with me. You don't need to go on."

James sighed. "Yes, you're right. I'm cross with you. I'm cross with you for being stupid. I'm cross with you for failing to see what a fool you're making of yourself."

Neil tried to remain calm. He could simply tell James to mind his own business—the temptation to do that was strong. But instead, he said, "Just leave it, James. Can't you see that I want to put it all behind me?"

James groaned. "Put what behind you? Her? The fact that you were the victim of a gross injustice?"

Neil did not reply immediately. Then he said, "I don't want to prolong any of it. I just don't."

"So you do nothing. Is that it? You just let it happen to you?"

Neil sighed. "I don't know."

James laughed. "You know all right. You know when the other person is the sort who will do it again. You know then. You know that if you let them get away with it, then that only means they'll go ahead and do it again. Or they think: I've got away with it. I've got away with it because this person who's forgiving me is going to let me do that, because he's too soft, or sentimental, or . . ." He hesitated.

"Go on," said Neil. "Or . . ."

"Or it's just sex. Because the other person is caught in the headlights of sex. Simple. People do stupid things because they can't help themselves. Everybody knows that. Sex overcomes reason. It's an old story. Story number one, in fact."

"I didn't say I was going back to her," said Neil, as calmly as he could. "All we did was talk." He wanted to point out that returning to Edinburgh was his affair, and that if he wanted advice he would ask for it, but he decided that would sound petty. And James, for all his tendency to interfere, had his best interests at heart—he knew that.

James shook his head. "I can't believe this," he said. "I really can't."

Neil became businesslike. "Do you mind? Do you mind if I stay with you in the flat for a few weeks? I'm going to look around for a job. Then I'll sort out somewhere to live."

James shrugged. "The room's there."

"You're very kind," said Neil.

"And you're very gullible."

James looked embarrassed. He had not meant to go so far. "I'm sorry," he muttered. "I shouldn't have said that."

Neil made a placatory gesture. "That's fine," he said.

"I'm right, of course," James went on.

"So am I," said Neil.

They looked at one another in silence. At last Neil said, "There's something I need to ask, James. Why have you been so fired up about what happened to me? I don't quite get it. I can understand that you didn't like seeing a friend treated in the way I was. But you seemed . . . well, incensed by it—far beyond what one might expect. And you couldn't see that I wanted just to get away from it. I don't really get it, I'm afraid."

James looked away. "Yes. Okay."

"Well? What does that mean?"

James sighed. "I don't like self-pity—I never have. But there's something that every gay person has to deal with, even today, when things are so much easier. There are still people who don't like you because of what you are. That's all there is to it."

"Surely not. Well, maybe there are some people, but nowadays . . ."

James was adamant. "No, it's true. You wouldn't know about it, but I'm telling you. I've had to deal with it. We all have. And I can tell you something: it hurts, because it's so unfair."

Neil made a gesture of acceptance. "All right. I understand. But what's that got to do with . . . with all this?"

"Everything," said James. "At least from where I am."

Neil looked puzzled.

"You see," James continued, "as you know, I was at a boarding school. I was bullied."

"We all meet bullies," said Neil.

"No, but you didn't have to . . . Sorry, special pleading, but there's a difference. I was really isolated. I was terribly lonely. And nobody seemed to see what was going on. It happens."

Neil said that he understood. "I didn't have to put up with what you did, I imagine."

"When I was young," James went on, "I used to tell myself that in spite of what I was going through, there had to be good people around—people who were kind. I looked for them, but for one reason or another they weren't there—or I was failing to find them. Then I got out of it. I got my place to study medicine and that was the big escape. I met you the first day of the course—remember? You may not, but I remember it well. And I thought, here's a good person."

When Neil looked away, James sensed that he had embarrassed him. "Sorry. I know you're modest. But that's what I felt."

"Oh well . . . Then you found out I can be as mean as the next person."

James laughed. "You wish. I thought: this guy is a good person. I saw how kind you were. And I thought: there are good people, and here's one. It was that simple. Hero worship, I suppose—something like that."

Neil felt himself blushing. "I don't know . . ."

"But it's true," James went on. "You are a good man, Neil. You just are. And when this blew up, I saw red. It's just the way it was. It suddenly became an example of how a good man can be shafted by scheming, ambitious people and by . . . I suppose by a sort of enthusiastic intolerance. I hated what I saw. I still do.

"And what made it worse was that I realised that the battle is more or less lost. You'd think that academia would be a place for people who insist on liberal values—who reject any sort of tyranny—but I don't think it is any longer. Let's not be naive about that."

James finished. He seemed embarrassed by the candour of what he had said. Now he continued, "I hadn't meant to burden you with all that, but you asked, didn't you?"

The following day, Neil drove into Tobermory to make a few purchases at the hardware store and to get supplies for the final few days in the cottage. He bought the groceries in the small Co-operative store on the front, opposite the sea wall, and then, with a copy of the *Scotsman* newspaper tucked under his arm he decided to walk to the harbour pontoons to look at the boats. There was a muster of sailing boats taking place, and a number of sleek yachts were tied up. Neil knew little about boats, but was beginning to understand the fascination that they held for Stuart, who could talk for hours about rigging and diesel engines and the intricacies of bilge pumps.

He saw Jill in the harbour car park. She had a life jacket slung over her arm, and was in the process of locking her car. She seemed surprised to see him.

"I thought that you'd gone back to Edinburgh," she said. "I saw James yesterday and he said . . ."

"Not yet," said Neil. "I'm going next week. Probably Tuesday."

She inclined her head. "I see."

Neil gestured to the life jacket. "You're going out?"

She said that she had a friend who owned a boat and she was going over to Kilchoan to look at a foal. "It's a lovely little thing," she said. "But something's putting it off its food."

"And it can't tell you, can it?"

She grinned. "My patients can tell me more than you imagine," she said. "It's just that they can't put it into words. But . . ."

She broke off. He waited.

"But what?"

"But it's the same with people," she said. "You can see what's troubling people without their ever having to say anything. Some silences are pretty eloquent."

He was bemused. The conversation was taking an unexpected direction. "You mean you can diagnose unhappiness? Or conflicting emotions, perhaps?"

She met his gaze. "Can't you? Can't you do that with your patients? I thought doctors developed that ability."

He shrugged. "I suppose an experienced GP can—after years and years of seeing people. I think they develop some sort of ability to see what's going on in the mind." He paused. "I'm not sure that I can, though. Or at least not yet. I'm not that sort of doctor. I'm interested in communicable diseases and living conditions and so on. That's not the touchy-feely end of medicine."

She pointed to a bench at the top of the walkway that led down to the pontoons. "We could sit down. I'm a bit early. Morna's always late, anyway. She doesn't wear a watch."

"She's given up time?"

Jill laughed. "Some of the people on this island have done that. They say that it's terrifically liberating."

They sat down on a rickety, blue-painted bench. Down below them, a small boat was manoeuvring its way into a berth. Seagulls soared and mewed above.

"You've been happy here?" she asked. "Here, on Mull?"

"Of course. I love it."

She fiddled with a strap of the life jacket. "But you couldn't stay?"

He hesitated. "No, I could. I think I could quite easily."

She seemed to reflect on this. "I suppose it depends on what you want from life. A place like this gives you some things—but not others."

"Like everywhere else, don't you think?"

She agreed. "You make a choice, don't you? You decide what you want out of life, and then you work out the compromises—which are always going to have to be made."

He looked at her. The wind blew a strand of hair off her brow. The skin of her forehead was brown from the sun. She worked in the open, of course—in fields, much of the time. And the weather here got everywhere, the salt breeze touched everything, stone, wood, skin, hair.

He asked her what she wanted out of life. "Since you raise the subject," he said, almost apologetically. "What do you want? If you don't mind talking about it."

"I don't mind talking about these things," she said. "A lot of people seem reluctant to go there, but I . . ."

"Well?"

She shrugged. "The usual things. I love luxury soaps."

He laughed. "That's quite an answer. What do you want out of life? Luxury soaps."

She laughed too. "Well, we all have our favourite ordinary things. I also go for cookery books—I collect them. And artichokes. I have a soft spot for artichokes and scrambled eggs, and anchovy paste. I can take or leave chocolate, but those savoury things are another matter altogether."

"And the bigger things?"

She looked thoughtful. "I suppose there's the work I do. That's the biggest thing in my life right now. I want to . . ." She looked down at the ground.

Neil encouraged her. "Go on."

"I want to ease the pain, I suppose. I see animal pain, and I want to do something about it. It goes with being a vet. If you don't want to do that, then I'm not sure you should be a vet."

He was silent. The gulls protested more shrilly. Then he said, "Of course. I can see that."

"There's so much pain in this world, isn't there? Everywhere you look, there's pain. Physical pain as well as the pain that comes with the unhappiness we inflict on one another."

She turned to him. "And you?"

"I'm not sure," he said. "I suppose I've been aware of what I don't want. That's not quite the same thing as knowing what you *do* want." He paused. This was not good enough. He wanted to say more, but he was having difficulty finding the words. He tried again. "We look for things that make sense for us, and we don't always find them. Then suddenly you realise what you're looking for, and there it is in front of you. It may have been there all the time."

"Of course."

He noticed that she had glanced at her watch. If he wanted to say more, he did not have much time to say it.

"Maybe . . ." he said.

"Yes?"

"Nothing."

Eighteen

It was a chance meeting. Neil had been back in Edinburgh for three days when he met Alice, the young woman from the institute administration. She said to him, "You're Dr. Anderson, aren't you?"

It took him a few seconds to recognise her, but then it came back to him. "Alice?"

"Yes. I work at—"

"Of course. Sorry, I've been away for a while."

"You were over on Skye, I heard."

"Mull."

"Yes, I heard that you'd gone over there. I have a brother who works on the ferries. I sometimes go over there. I went to Barra last year."

The encounter took place in a supermarket on Morningside Road. It was early evening, and was quiet. Neil noticed that Alice was laden with cat provisions. "I can see who's eating you out of house and home," he remarked, pointing to the packets of expensive cat treats she had selected.

"He's Siamese," she said. "They have fancy tastes."

She smiled. Then, her voice lowered, she said, "I heard what happened. I'm sorry."

He hesitated. He had not been sure exactly of who knew of his suspension and its connection with his subsequent resignation. She must have known because she processed contracts and salaries. She would know everything, he imagined.

"That's kind of you," he said. "It's behind me now, of course."

She looked uncomfortable. "It shouldn't be. You'd done nothing wrong—at least that's the version I heard."

"I don't think I did anything," he said. "But that's the world we live in, I suppose."

Alice considered this. "Yes, but it can be very unfair. Anybody can accuse anybody of anything. It doesn't matter what the truth is."

Neil shrugged. "There's not much anybody can do, I'm afraid."

Alice looked thoughtful. "She's a hypocrite," she said.

"Who?"

"The boss. Henrietta. She's dishonest."

Neil was careful. "I did hear something," he said.

Alice's eyes flashed with anger. "You heard something because I found out what was going on. But nobody wants to do anything about it, and it's hard for me. If you're the junior person, you end up getting the blame yourself. They try to fire you. They call you a whistleblower and then that's it."

"I know what you mean," said Neil. "It's not easy."

Alice was getting into her stride. "I went to two people who were senior to me. Two. First of all, I went to that microbiologist woman, Chrissie Thomson. I knew her a bit, and she'd been kind to me when I broke up with my boyfriend. I told her all about it. I gave her a copy of the falsified claim. She said that she'd do something about it, but she didn't come back to me. I went to Alan—you know him? He's a toxicologist. A nice man. He said he'd pass it on to you. That's the last I heard of it."

"I see."

"Chrissie came to see me. She asked me who I'd told about this.

I said that I'd spoken to Alan, and he said that he was going to speak to you."

Neil was reeling at the disclosure. She had told Chrissie, and Chrissie had not mentioned it to him. Not once. She knew—and she knew that he, too, knew.

"I suppose I just have to get used to it," Alice went on. "You can't get justice in this life. Maybe I shouldn't be so naive about these things."

Neil looked at, his watch. "I have to get some things for dinner," he said. "Do you mind?"

"I have to get on too," said Alice. "I hope we see one another again some time."

"I hope so too," said Neil.

Chrissie telephoned.
"You don't mind my calling, do you?" she said.

He replied that he did not. But he did; he knew that she would contact him, but had not been looking forward to it. For a moment he hesitated: now was the time to tell her that he no longer wished to speak to her, but, out of ancient habit, he said nothing. He was courteous by instinct, unable to hurt.

"Because I was worried that you might not want to speak to me," she continued.

"I don't mind."

He heard the intake of breath. But what had she expected from him?

"That doesn't sound very friendly," she said.

"I'm not sure that we're friends," he said.

"That sounds even less friendly."

He said nothing.

Then she continued, "I wondered whether you'd like to come round for dinner. Just for dinner."

He hesitated; but then, "All right." He imagined what James might say to him, but he put the thought of that out of his mind.

Now, with a wedge of Parmesan and a bottle of Chianti in a tote bag, he stood before the familiar door. He could see the place where there had been a sticker with his name written on it for the postman, now removed. He rang the bell.

She stood before him. She had washed her hair and it was imperfectly dry. "I look a bit like a drowned rat," she said. "I'll need a few minutes."

He stepped past her. "Not going to give me a kiss?" she said.

He stopped. It would be churlish to decline. But he did not kiss her on the lips.

He could see that she could tell there was something wrong. "Are you all right?" she asked.

"Yes."

"You don't sound it."

He took a deep breath. "Actually, I'm not."

She gestured for him to follow her into the living room. "Everybody's going down with some bug. You're probably brewing that. There were twenty fewer students at my lecture this morning. All down with it, I was told. Of course, these things spread like wildfire in the student body; they're always kissing one another—what can they expect?"

She seemed to expect him to find this amusing, but he turned away.

"Neil? Are you sure you're up to dinner? Do you want to go back to James's place?"

He put the cheese down on the table. "Maybe I won't eat."

"I can give you an aspirin. Or ibuprofen. I find that ibuprofen works for me."

"It's not that," said Neil. "I don't feel physically ill."

She frowned. "Is something upsetting you?"

He had not intended this. He had thought they would have a distant, polite dinner, but suddenly he knew that he had to speak out. It had not been a good idea to come.

"Human behaviour," he said. "The way people act. The things they do to others."

"What?"

He turned back to face her. He wanted to watch her reaction to what he was about to say. "There's a woman called Alice in administration," he began. "You know her. She knows you. She spoke to you about something that she had discovered. Do you remember that?"

He knew immediately that it was true. Chrissie opened her mouth to say something, but then closed it again without uttering a word.

"What I'd like to know," he said, "is why you didn't say anything to me about Henrietta when you know—you *knew*—that I'd been told about the false expenses claim. You didn't say anything. Why?"

She struggled to speak. "It was . . . I'm . . ."

He shook his head. "You knew. *You knew.* You knew that Alan was going to leave it to me to make an official complaint about this. You knew that the people on the inside didn't want to do it. And so you must have decided—you and Henrietta, I think—must have decided that I had to be kept on side. So, how to guarantee that I did nothing to rock the boat? If you and I got together again, then that would sort all that out—for the time being. You felt confident that you'd be able to persuade me from confronting Henrietta— because Henrietta was your friend. That's why you came over to Mull. That's why you decided to try to rekindle our relationship."

He had expected her to protest—to interrupt him. But she remained silent.

"I was surprised that you and Henrietta became so close," he said. "Can't you see through her?"

She shook her head. "You'll never understand. Henrietta is just doing what men have done for ages. She's playing men at their own game. But she has to be strong to get anywhere."

He shook his head. "Does past inequality give women like her a free pass? Does it justify what she did?"

Chrissie's eyes narrowed. "Past inequality? Do you really think that's all over? Do you really think that women no longer have to battle for everything they have?" She paused. "If you think that, Neil, we're not living in the same world."

"But she doesn't care about the truth," he retorted. "Or am I being old-fashioned?"

Chrissie allowed herself a smile. "I'm tempted to answer: yes."

"She recruited you," he said. "You wanted my job, didn't you? You envied me. You encouraged me to stand up to Henrietta so that she would suspend me. You pretended to sympathise with me. You used me."

She stared at him, but did not say anything. He had been as explicit as he could. And he knew that what he had said had struck home, because she did not deny it. After some moments of silence she said, "What now?"

He waited. It was still possible to change the plan that he had made, but he decided that he did not want to do that.

"I'm not going to report her," he said.

It took a few moments for this to sink in. Then she visibly relaxed. "That's probably for the best."

"I think she should be given the chance to resign," he continued.

Her lower lip quivered. "Resign?"

"Not altogether," said Neil. "Just from her director's post. She'll still have her lecturing job. That's enough for plenty of people—

she might reflect on that for a time. She doesn't need to direct any-thing." He paused. "I'm giving her a chance. Can't you see that?"

Chrissie nodded—reluctantly.

"I'm going to see her tomorrow," Neil went on. "I'm going to say to her that if she resigns, nobody will mention her false expenses claims." Then he added, "I might also point out to her that it would be a good idea for her to confirm that the accusations against me weren't supported by sufficient evidence—which happens to be true."

She started to say something, but he continued, "The way I'll put it will be to say to her that everybody deserves a second chance. I'm going to give her that chance."

Chrissie was silent. Then she asked, "Why are you doing this?"

"The world's in a sorry mess," Neil said. "People put so much energy into finding fault with others, with attacking them, with cal-culating personal advantage, with . . . with all of those things. We've broken the bonds that exist between us, with the result that we are all potential enemies of one another, locked in mutual suspicion and distrust. And do you know what? I've had enough of it. I can't bear to be part of that any longer."

She listened to him without moving. She looked impassive.

"I hope that you aren't unhappy," he said. "I hope that ambition doesn't wreck your life. I hope that you find somebody you can be faithful to."

She looked at him, but remained silent.

"We were never in love, were we?" he said.

She shook her head. "No, I don't think we were. I liked you, though . . ."

"Yes, and I suppose I liked you." He paused. "But I wasn't enough for you, was I?"

She looked away.

"Go on," he said. "Can't you at least admit it?"

She turned to face him. "What do you want me to say? That I got tired of you?"

"If that's what happened, yes."

She made a *leave me alone* gesture. "It did."

He felt curiously immune to her words. So what if he bored her? She bored him. They bored each other. "All right."

And then she said, "Would it help if I said that I'm sorry?"

"You already said that."

"This time I mean it."

He hesitated. He looked about the room in which they were standing. He looked through the window, with its view of Arthur's Seat in the distance, the hill that watched over Edinburgh, just visible above the roofs with their grey stone and their rows of chimney pots. He saw the evening sky behind the shoulders of the hill, a sky that was light blue and tolerant. The moon could just be made out, sailing pale and white, traced against the emptiness, indifferent to our dramas down below. He remembered walking down the track after dinner at Maddy's and seeing it much brighter, hanging over Mull like a watchful night light.

"It helps to know that—of course it helps. But I think it's best for me to go. Sometimes it is."

She went with him to the door, where she kissed him on the cheek and gave his hand a quick clasp of the sort that friends will exchange when they leave one another—one of those tiny, subtle gestures of friendship that now meant little, and tasted of nothing at all.

A week later, he was back on Mull. James was in Edinburgh, but had put the house at his disposal once again. "Paint the back door," he said. "That's all I ask of you. And a drain might need unblocking. Oh, and the guttering—if you could clear it out at the front. Apart from that . . ."

They had both laughed. Then James went on, "Not that I should tell you what to do. I think you've had enough of that."

"I've always appreciated your advice," Neil assured him. "Even if I haven't always followed it."

"You've never followed it," said James. "Except, I suppose, you did stand up to Henrietta. Eventually."

"I'm pleased you acknowledge that."

"In a way," James added. "She still got away with it—to an extent. I would have gone for the jugular."

Neil shook his head. "Punishing other people often amounts to punishing yourself. Have you ever thought of that?"

"Of course, you're the great philosopher." James laughed. "About that door . . . the paint's in the shed, but you may need to get more from that hardware shop in Tobermory, the one that sells whisky as well as buckets and stuff."

"I'll do all that," said Neil.

"And I'll come over in a couple of weeks' time—just for a few days. To check up on you. People can go to Mull and turn all strange, you know."

"We'll see," said Neil.

Now he was sitting in Maddy and Stuart's house on a Saturday. It was shortly after twelve, and Maddy was slicing potatoes. Stuart was on his tractor, just visible on the hillside, carting something about on what he referred to as cattle business. Neil was looking up at the ceiling, which bore the signs of an ancient leak from somewhere above. He would offer to paint their ceiling, he thought: it was the least one might do for people who had become such good friends.

Maddy said, "That's it," and swept the last slices of potato into a bowl. "Potatoes are so . . . so unambitious."

Neil laughed. "That's a wonderful observation," he said.

"Thank you. But it's true, I think. Potatoes have never really inspired many metaphors, have they? Unlike flowers."

"True."

"Flowers have a whole language, don't they? Or we attribute a language to them."

Neil remembered a book on the language of flowers that his mother had. "People used them to send messages, didn't they? Each flower had a particular meaning, and you could use them to spell out what you had in mind."

"Yes," said Maddy. "But I think the language of flowers is one of those languages that's dying out. Like those languages in New Guinea or wherever that disappear each year as the last speaker dies. Imagine being the last speaker of a language? Think of what it must be like."

Neil said that it would obviously be lonely. It would always be lonely, he thought, if you had stories to tell that nobody would understand.

Maddy had been taking plates out of a cupboard. She paused, and put the plates down. "What would it be like without stories?"

"Dull," answered Neil. "Dull, and dangerous."

The dangerousness made her think. He was right, she thought. And now she said, "And it would be dangerous without poets, wouldn't it."

Neil agreed. "Probably."

"Poetry has such a clear voice, after all," Maddy said. "It distils things. Boils them down. And suddenly there it is: the truth in a few well-chosen words.

"I looked at some Auden this morning," she said. "I had ten minutes before I had to go and see to the goats. So I sat down and read something that I go back to time and time again. You might know it."

"I doubt it."

"It's a very short poem he wrote called 'The More Loving One.' And I remember it because it sets out what could be an entire philosophy of life in a couple of lines. *If equally affection cannot be, Let the more loving one be me."*

"That's it?"

She smiled. "There are a few other lines, but yes, those are the important ones. What he means is that we should give more love to the world than we may get in return. But it also means that you start the process of healing and reconciliation and so on by giving love. You have to make the first move. That's the way I read it, anyway." She paused, and looked directly at Neil. "I think that you're somebody who understands that. A lot of people don't, but I think you do."

He did not respond, and she went on to ask, "You've done something about a job?"

"I spoke to them at the medical practice. They're very keen. There are two medical posts here—available immediately."

"And—"

"I have a bit of maintenance to do first . . ."

She smiled at that. He had spoken about the doors and the guttering.

"And I need to look for a place of my own," he continued. "I'm going to see something down at Salen."

"I hope that works out."

She looked at the clock on the wall. Neil intercepted her glance. Then he looked out of the window. He had a good view of the farm road that led to the house, and he would be able to see Jill's car as it approached. He tried to remember when he had last done this— watched for the arrival of somebody, willing her to come, knowing that more than anything else he wanted to see her, to be with her. It was a litmus test that was rarely wrong.

"Jill hoped to get here at about twelve thirty," he said. "She told me she has a couple of calls to make. A horse with a sore foot. And a cat that's been fighting again."

"Good. Lunch will be ready at one, or thereabouts."

Maddy knew. She knew, of course, and he realised that she knew. Now they looked at one another in sympathy. Understanding did not always require words, Neil thought.

Maddy turned to Neil.

"Fortunate man," she said.

"Why?"

She held his gaze in complete candour. They were concealing nothing from one another. "Because of her," she said. "Because of her—and a great deal else."

He looked out at the sky. There were wisps of cloud, dashes of white, moving fast, carried by the winds from further west. And then, as he lowered his gaze, he saw Jill's car coming down the track. He stood up, and smiled.

A B O U T   T H E   A U T H O R

Alexander McCall Smith is the author of The No. 1 Ladies' Detective Agency novels and of a number of other series and stand-alone books. His works have been translated into more than forty languages and have been bestsellers throughout the world. He lives in Scotland.